Jessie

master bedroom.

The amphibians returned, playing leapfrog in her middle. She stared at Corbin's bed. "You don't expect us to share that, do you?"

Corbin rested his forearm against the other side of the doorframe. His mouth rose in a curious smile as he looked from the bed to her. "Uh, yeah. That's what husbands and wives usually do."

"But you haven't even held my hand!" Her voice came across stronger than normal.

Corbin turned and leaned his back against the frame, narrowing the space between them. "You want me to … hold your hand?"

Fully indignant, Jessie squared her jaw and faced him. "If you expect to hold anything else, that would be a good place to start."

Books by Regina Tittel

Abandoned Hearts

Unexpected Kiss

Coveted Bride

Cherished Stranger

Devoted Mission

Love for Lenore

Rivalry & Romance

Fourth Time's the Charm

Conveniently Yours

Regina Tittel

After the Vows series

Book One

CONVENIENTLY YOURS

Published by Regina Tittel
Copyright © 2015 by Regina Tittel
Cover design by Regina Tittel
Photograph by Regina Tittel

All Scripture quotations are taken from the King James Version.

ISBN-13: 978-1511625494
ISBN-10: 151162549X

Regina Tittel's books are written to uplift and encourage each individual while also entertaining them with a great story.

"Peace I leave with you, my peace I give unto you: not as the world giveth, give I unto you. Let not your heart be troubled, neither let it be afraid."

–John 14:27

A big thank you goes to my family—they not only encourage me but give me lots of material! (The mints were worth it, Jerad!)

Thank you, Candace and J. L., for your patience while posing for the cover. You're not only a beautiful couple but great to work with.

Always, thank you, God, for making this possible.

Chapter One

"I'm sorry, please give me a moment." Jessie Thompson returned the insufficient cash to her wallet and retrieved a credit card. She'd always thought it wrong to use credit for groceries, yet now had no other choice.

"No, no, I've got this."

She turned to the familiar voice of her neighbor, Corbin Vaughn, and frowned. "What are you doing? You're not buying my groceries."

"Buying groceries with a credit card? Never a good idea."

She despised being treated as if she didn't know better—like an irresponsible youth.

Corbin's arm brushed past her as he handed his money to the cashier. "Just add my deli order to hers." He glanced at Jessie with a look of disapproval. "We'll settle up when we get home."

"When we—you make it sound like we're married," she hissed.

The clerk's penciled in eyebrows perked with interest.

"Which we're not. We're neighbors."

"Uh-huh." The woman didn't sound convinced.

"He has his house. I have mine." Jessie was rambling and knew it. Why of all checkout lines did she have to choose this woman's register? Her reserved expression came across accusing. What did she think—that Jessie and Corbin were having an affair!

God help me, I shouldn't even care what the woman thinks. It was Corbin's fault and his constant way of making her feel inferior.

In a sudden rush for time, Jessie left the warmth of the store and pushed her cart through the automatic door. She pulled her coat together to block the instant chill. The smooth tile beneath her feet changed to rough pavement as she hurried toward her car.

Corbin caught up with her in the parking lot. "Do I need to pay you more?"

"No—of course not. It wouldn't even feel right. I love your kids." Jessie watched Corbin's two children after school and throughout the summer. His pay was fair. *Life* wasn't.

A car honked as it passed. Jessie waved without looking then pointed at Corbin's overstuffed deli bag with a smirk. "Besides, with the way you eat, I doubt you could afford it."

"Very funny. I got lunch for the crew." He withdrew an individually wrapped sandwich with his burly hand and pulled down a corner of the paper wrapping. With one bite, half the sandwich disappeared. He mumbled around his food, "You have to try this."

Before she could smart-off another comment, he shoved the sandwich into her mouth.

He swallowed and asked, "Are you having problems?" Despite his chauvinistic ways, Corbin did care.

"I'm fine. Great." She spoke while trying to manage the mouthful of food. The flavor of the sandwich sparked her taste buds to life. "And so is that. What is it?"

"Deluxe ham salad. Here," he pressed the remainder in her hand, "finish it off. I have a couple more."

He reached for a bag to load into her car, but she waved him off. "From the looks of your purchase, your crew's waiting on lunch. I can load this. It isn't much."

"If you say so." He frowned and stepped back.

Had she offended him? Probably. He always offered a hand, and she always refused. Not that it helped. Corbin would get his way when he really wanted to. Just like in the grocery store.

Moments later Jessie pulled into her well-kept suburb, and out of habit, glanced past her house down the street toward Corbin's. Why did she always do that? More than likely for comfort. Since her husband died two years ago, Corbin was the one person in her life that provided any source of . . . what—protection, security? It didn't make sense. They fought over everything, but even that was better than the emptiness of widowhood.

She put the groceries away in a hurried mess. The day had sped by leaving little time for work, though after turning on the computer she'd had little reason to fret. Still no buyers. Jessie searched through the photos of antiques she'd listed. The pictures were good, clear, and caught the different angles of each piece.

In another window, she opened her email and typed, "Tara, how's your sales? Are they down like mine?"

Tara Holden, Jessie's best friend and beautician for the past ten years, had helped her start a part-time business. But there wasn't any security flipping antiques. One day the market would be hot with buyers, the next a freeze.

***

"Hi Mom!"

"Jessie, we're home."

Jessie glanced at the clock on her computer. Where had the time gone? "I'm coming." She left the office and greeted each child with a hug. "How was your day?" She directed her question to include everyone.

Shannon Vaughn jumped up and down. "I got the part I wanted in the Christmas play!"

Jessie's heart leaped with excitement. "You're the orphan girl—the main character?" She'd never won a leading role during her school years. Pride welled inside her for the shy eleven-year old.

"No, I didn't want that. I changed my mind."

For the last month, Shannon had worried over the most important role. Perplexed, Jessie asked, "Then what part did you get?"

"Lead singer." Shannon glowed with the announcement.

"Wow!"

"And she singed to me on the way home."

"Sang." Jessie corrected her six-year-old daughter, Layla.

Not long after, the boys called for help. Jessie stepped outside to see what mess they'd gotten into this time. Her Timmy, and Shannon's brother, Garret, were both eight and possessed way too much creativity when together.

Great. The Frisbee had landed on the roof. Though not the trouble she'd expected, still, she wasn't sure how to get it down. "I don't know guys, but I'll give it a try." She walked to the garage, shaking her head. *Isn't Frisbee a summer sport? What are they doing playing it now?*

The ladder hadn't been put to use in years. She considered the ten foot frame hanging in the garage. How would she wrestle it out on her own? An image of Corbin handling the job with ease ignited her determination. She didn't need another reason to rely on him—and fuel his . . . his what? What was it about Corbin Vaughn that built resentment in her? True, he would be able to do the job easier than her. True, she hadn't wanted to pay with the credit card. But relying on him made her feel small.

Jessie stood inside the garage and stared at the wall. She needed a ladder just to reach the ladder.

"Mom, maybe we should just leave it."

"Yeah, Jessie, let's just wait for my dad. He can fix anything."

Her spine stiffened. "Well so can I. Move back, boys, and watch what a woman can do."

Once the boys were safely to the side, she backed her van out then drove into the garage again, closer to the wall. From the front bumper, she climbed onto the hood then the roof of the automobile. "Easy, peasy." Full of confidence, Jessie grabbed the ladder and hoisted it from the wall brackets. It was heavier than she realized. The weight caused her to teeter on top the car. One glance between the wall and the car confirmed she couldn't let go. Paint thinner and who knew what else lined the shelf.

With a deep breath, she turned around. One end of the ladder caught another shelf and scattered boxes on the floor of the garage. "Oops."

Giggles erupted from the young glee club. "Thanks for your support, boys. Later you can help me clean up." She lowered an end of the ladder. The weight rushed the extension forward, obnoxiously clicking past the rung locks until the aluminum slid against her front bumper, grating against the finish. *Lovely*.

She glanced at the wide eyes of the boys. "Not a word to your dad, Garret, okay?"

He nodded as if he understood. Hopefully, he did.

Full steam ahead, Jessie dragged the over-sized tool to the side of the house and propped it up.

"Mom, that's not even." Timmy pointed to the lop-sided ladder.

The lawn on the side of the house slanted downhill. Jessie chewed the inside of her lip and glanced around the yard. Given this particular suburb's rules, the area was immaculate. Not even a rock to use under the ladder.

Garret ran from the garage. "Will this work?" Held in his palm was a wedge used to hold back a door. Leave it to the general contractor's son to find a solution.

"Perfect." Jessie slipped it beneath a foot of the ladder. Checking its balance with her hands, she climbed to the porch roof. Only when she reached the top, did she realize she should've moved the ladder over a foot. Not a problem, she could reach.

Her fingers brushed against the Frisbee. *Almost there.* Leaning out a little more, Jessie's confidence grew. There were a lot of things she never thought she could do until becoming a single parent. She stretched a little farther.

"Aha! Got it." In her excitement, her precarious perch teetered to the side. Jessie grasped at the shingled roof with one hand while the other clung to the prized saucer. She'd almost righted herself when her hand slipped.

The ladder slid downward along the overhang, scraping and creaking against the shingle edges. Realizing her doom, Jessie let go of the Frisbee and snatched at the roof, but momentum was against her. The yell that followed would've sounded more like a scream, if not for her pride. She braced herself for the impact that would more than likely involve entanglement with the ladder ... and a broken leg.

"Oof!" Her landing came sooner than expected, followed by the sound of the ladder slapping the ground. "Corbin?"

"Of all the crazy notions." He promptly set her on her feet. "You don't have any business on a ladder."

A surge of anger colored her words. "And who made you king of my palace? When I want your opinion, I'll ask for it." She felt the heat in her face as much as the bruises caused from falling into his rock-hard arms.

"I have a right to state my opinion when the woman I've trusted to watch my children tries to break her neck." He hefted the ladder off the lawn with one hand and disappeared inside the garage.

Why did they always argue? Jessie sighed and picked up the mail scattered on the lawn. Corbin had probably dropped it on his way to her rescue. He often brought her mail in when picking up his kids. She figured it was more from curiosity than courtesy.

She shuffled through the contents as she climbed to the porch. One envelope was of particular interest. She tore the end off, ripping through the return address of her bank and plopped on the top step.

"Bad news?" Corbin was beside her, changing in an instant from a drill sergeant barking orders to a kind and compassionate friend.

Jessie read through the formal jargon already knowing what it would say. "I guess you need to know." She sighed, all fight slipping from her body. "Since the car broke down, then the refrigerator, and I don't remember what else, I fell behind on my payments.

"Without Richard's paycheck, I can't afford this house." She waved toward her home. "It's too big for us anyway."

"What are you saying?"

Jessie could feel his imploring eyes searching for an explanation. She chanced a look beside her at the man who'd been a constant part of her life for the last few years. A surprised emotion flickered across her heart. She'd miss fighting with him. "I have a buyer for the house. They've always wanted it."

"What?" His mouth moved in a silent stutter. "Where will you go?"

She shrugged. "I'll find a place in town. I've spotted a few apartments."

Corbin was shaking his head before she even finished. "You can't live in an apartment. You're a house person. Your kids have been raised here—in this small subdivision—they wouldn't know how to behave in an apartment complex."

Now he was irritating again.

"What do you mean they wouldn't know how to behave? What do you think I'm raising? Baboons?

"No, but they feel safe here. What if they're too trusting and you find out one of your neighbors has a criminal record?"

She rose, and he followed her inside. His ease in her home didn't surprise her. She'd watched his kids since before her husband passed.

"What if they start hanging with a bad group of kids?"

"Stop. What you're really upset about is losing your babysitter."

"This is ridiculous. Why are we even doing this?"

"Wow." This had to be the first time he'd backed down. But he should. This wasn't any of his business. "I'm glad you finally came to that realization. After all, this is my life."

"No. I mean why are we doing this?" He gestured between them and the basement toward the sound of the children. "We should just get married. Then we wouldn't have to worry about," he slapped the bank paper she still held, "all that."

"Are you crazy?" She stared at him, trying to catch a glimpse of humor. His eyes were steady. He wasn't joking. "All we do is fight." She turned to gather his kids' school bags.

"I know a good way to settle this." He called down the basement steps. "Hey all you monkeys, come up here and answer a question for me."

Like a herd of elephants, footsteps clamored up the steps while Jessie's heart plummeted to her feet. He wouldn't. He couldn't.

He did.

"What would you kids think if I married Jessie and we became a family?"

Jessie rounded the corner of the hallway to hear a resounding cheer. Shannon was the first to hug her. "Now I can call you Mom like they do!"

Trouble didn't begin to describe what Jessie was in.

Shannon pulled away and hoisted Layla into the air. "And you'll be my little sister!"

The boys cheered in unison. Jessie turned to the instigator. Her head pounded with a force she wanted to unleash on him. "Corbin, may I have a word with you?"

"Sorry, Shannon has a dentist appointment. We'll talk later." He called for Garret and herded his kids out the door.

Coward!

"Mom, I didn't know you and Corbin liked each other. That's great. Now Garret and me will be brothers."

Not if I wring his neck first.

Chapter Two

"Tara, how can I marry him? He gets on my every nerve." Jessie slumped back in the booth after sharing yesterday's details with her best friend. The fries she'd consumed in a nervous haste settled heavily in her gut.

Tara's gay-hearted laugh proved she wasn't convinced of the impossible situation. "I don't see you have much of a choice."

"Of course I have a choice." A rush of indignation warmed Jessie's cheeks. "I can support us fine, just . . . with a smaller house."

"And you'll do great, even though you have no previous skill set, you'll still have those other payments to meet and less income because of the loss of your babysitting job. Not to mention how this might affect his children." She took a long drink from her glass of sweet-tea.

Tara was right. How could she keep up rent and bills without the extra income from Corbin? Her throat tightened. Memories of the past painted a haunting possibility. Her mother had lost her job and then her home. They'd lived out of their car for over a year. Jessie wouldn't put her children through that.

"Stop frowning. The marriage makes sense. You've known him and have watched his kids for several years. What's so wrong with it?"

Despite the risks, how could she go through with the marriage? Corbin didn't love her. Not that she had any real feelings for him either. Her mind stalled at the thought, but she chose to ignore it. "You know how chauvinistic he is."

"Um … no."

"Okay," Jessie ran her fingers through her hair. "He talks like women can't do anything. Like when I was getting the Frisbee off the roof, or pressure washing the house. And the time I was charging the car battery!" She wadded the napkin in her hand.

"So … because he caught you when you fell off the ladder and he had the gall to turn the pressure down before the water ate a pattern of squiggles on the vinyl siding? And because he kept you from shocking yourself with the battery?" She tapped a long finger on the edge of her glass. "I see your point. Total male-chauvinist."

"You weren't there so don't defend him. What he didn't say—which wasn't much—his body language said for him." Jessie wrinkled her nose and huffed. "You're supposed to be on my side."

"Well then, in all reality, you could probably find a job that pays enough to get by. But with so little time left before you have to be out of your house, do you want to take that risk? Also, if you were truly honest with yourself, I think you'd admit to feelings for the guy."

Jessie gasped, "Are you crazy?"

"I've known you a long time. There's definitely something there." Tara glanced at her watch. "As much as I've enjoyed this live, romance audio, I have to head back to work."

She reached over and gave Jessie a quick hug. "You should answer yes. It'll all work out."

Jessie watched Tara leave, unable to grasp her lack of support. "You weren't any help," she hollered in retort. Other patrons turned toward her with curious glances. Jessie gathered her purse and rummaged for a tip. Let them stare, it was better than trying to explain her situation and having them agree with Tara.

After returning home, Jessie punched her computer on. "Yes!" An email revealed she'd made a sale of one-hundred-fifty dollars for a set of Corning Ware cookware. The money would cover this month's electric bill as long as the temperature didn't take a drastic drop.

She printed out the address of the buyer and marked the product sold. Her fingers thrummed on top of the desk while waiting for the printed label. Slowly, her hand became still. The desk had been her grandfather's. Solid oak, the wood had aged beautifully leaving dark lines trailing in the grain. For a moment, she wondered how much the desk would bring before coming to her senses. She could sell every piece of furniture she had and still be looking for a paycheck in a couple of months.

God, I need something steady. But even as the prayer left her thoughts, she didn't want lifestyle to change. She loved working from home, watching Corbin's children, and not answering to anyone.

Was that why she didn't want to remarry? She pulled her mouth to the side in thought. She'd loved being married to Richard, living the day to day life of raising children and doing things for him. A pain shot through her heart. If it weren't for his car accident, she'd still enjoy life as his wife.

With Corbin, everything was different. They were just neighbors, not a dating couple. Not even a blip on the radar screen. Which is why the possibility seemed so outlandish.

Yet, one she still considered.

The day rolled by in a predicted haze. After school, she blocked the children's constant chatter from her mind and concentrated on driving to church where Corbin would meet them like he did every Wednesday.

"Good, we're early." She turned to address Shannon and the three faces seated in the back. "I want all of you to take a seat once we're inside while I visit with the pastor." A round of nodding heads acknowledged they'd heard her.

Inside, the comforting smell of lemon and pine greeted her like an old friend. She walked beneath the timber framed ceiling and past the pulpit, her shoes clicking against the polished hardwood floor. Pastor Wade was busy in the choir practice room which had temporarily been turned into a pantry. Lined against the wall were several flats of food that had been dropped off in preparation for Thanksgiving.

Jessie's stomach tightened and threatened to steal her confidence. But she had to talk to him. As a man of God, he would see the situation for what it was and talk sense into both her and Corbin.

"Pastor Wade."

He jerked up from counting the cans, causing Jessie to jump back. "Oh, hi. Didn't realize I had company. Did you have something to donate to the shelter?"

"Actually no," Jessie swallowed the lump in her throat. "I need some advice."

He glanced at his watch before leading her to the folding chairs against the wall. "What is it?"

She always appreciated how this busy man slowed down for anyone in need, but now that she had his undivided attention, Jessie struggled with where to begin. "For the last couple of years, things have been a little tight at home, but we've managed to get by." She cleared her throat. "But more recently, that's all changed. Because of a few breakdowns and such, I fell behind on my house payments."

"I'm sorry. I didn't know." Concern marred her pastor's brow.

"And that's my fault, because I didn't want to be a burden to anyone." The pastor tried to speak but she plowed ahead, knowing if she didn't she'd find herself agreeing to accepting money from the church, something she couldn't do in good conscience. If she wasn't able to work it would be different. Despite knowing she could probably make more money with a steady job, she'd stubbornly chosen not to work outside the house.

"All of that was to say, I'm about to lose my house …" a cascade of emotion threatened to break free as the fact was spoken aloud, "and Corbin has asked me to marry him."

A mixture of responses played across Pastor Wade's face. "I'm sorry to hear about your house, but that's wonderful news about you and Corbin." He paused in his evident approval and peered closer. "Or is it not?"

"I don't think it's wise to marry just to solve my money problems."

A smile slid across his face. "No, I wouldn't think so either. But you aren't marrying only for those reasons. When do you want me to perform the ceremony?"

Jessie blinked and shook her head. "You're not listening. I can't marry someone who doesn't love me."

This time, the man actually laughed. "Jessie, Corbin has—"

"Pastor Wade," Mavis Gardner, well-known church gossip, entered with a jug of apple cider. "Well hello, Jessie, didn't mean to intrude on your *counseling*. I'll just leave this here beside the canned food and let you be."

She paused in the door way. "It's time for church to start. And Jessie, you know you can always come to me, dear, if you need anything."

Jessie forced her upper lip to move in a semblance of a smile. *Only if I want the whole town to know.* She turned back to the pastor. This week wasn't going as well as she'd planned.

"We'd better go, too, then. Let's say a prayer before we leave." The pastor bowed his head.

Leave? He hadn't finished what he'd been about to say. He hadn't told her not to marry Corbin.

"… and bless the union of these special people. I can't think of two better suited for marriage, and thank you, for finally opening their eyes."

Jessie moved methodically back to the sanctuary. The children were out of their seats, running and hiding between pews even as more members arrived to take their seats. Her mouth tightened in aggravation. They knew better—Corbin stood where the children were supposed to be seated, his back to their mischievous acts.

She rolled her eyes. If he was serious about becoming a father to four, he should be exercising his parenting skills not talking to … a sway of light colored hair reflected in the fluorescent light.

Great. Alyssa Halpin.

Jessie made her way down the aisle as Alyssa turned to go to the choir loft. Glowing, the younger woman smiled brightly at first then, as if realizing who Jessie was, narrowed her eyes.

Jessie brushed off the unfriendly act. She'd never understood Alyssa's distant attitude and wasn't about to worry about it now. "Kids, take your seats." One by one, her and Corbin's children stopped their play and scooted down their usual pew.

Layla patted a vacant seat between her and Shannon. "Sit between us, Mommy."

Jessie did as requested. Corbin turned from talking to yet another member who'd stepped inside. Instead of sitting behind them as he often did, he surprised Jessie by joining them in the same pew.

She had to acknowledge his presence, but didn't know what to say. Like the tin man in need of oil, her neck turned with reluctance until finally resting on the man seated one child over.

He repositioned himself, casting an arm over the back of the pew. His fingers brushed against her shoulder for the briefest moment. "Did you have a good day?"

Jessie rolled her eyes before focusing forward again. "No."

From her side view, she saw Corbin's mouth tilt in humor as he shook his head. He thought this was funny? The man was blind. But as soon the service ended, she'd enlighten him.

From the choir, Alyssa straightened her robe over her tall, slim figure then cast a glance toward Corbin. She had her sites set … no wonder she didn't like Jessie.

A spiral of irritation wound around her spine. Jessie reconsidered. The conversation wouldn't be had here. Too many interested parties.

***

At the end of service, those who would be working at the shelter were asked to remain. As church members mingled on their way out, Jessie turned and hid herself in conversation with the children. With Corbin sharing their pew, there was sure to be speculation over their relationship, and she couldn't bring herself to look her church family in the eye.

"Dad's going to marry Jessie!"

"Shannon!" Jessie turned and, to her instant relief, saw only one member standing by their pew. "We're, err, discussing the idea."

"That's nice. You'll make a lovely family."

Corbin smiled. "Yeah, Jess, we'll make a lovely family."

The woman patted Corbin's shoulder before moving on. "She's such a sweet lady. Take good care of her."

Jessie shrunk down in the pew. *Could this day get any worse?*

Once Pastor Wade finished shaking congregants' hands, he returned to the front. He cleared his throat, and for one panicking instant, Jessie feared he would announce her and Corbin's engagement. A surge of relief washed over her when he, instead, brought up the subject of the shelter.

"As most of you know, the renovation of the old community hall is nearing completion. We did find a section of floor still needing replaced. That, and painting the partitioning wall. I believe Corbin Vaughn has volunteered to repair the floor. And Jessie, you did such a nice job painting the kitchen, would you be willing to tackle the last painting project?"

"I'll probably be out there anyway with … err … yes. That's not a problem." Her face heated with the almost mention of Corbin's name. She kept her focus forward, not wanting to endure Corbin's gloating.

After the meeting, Jessie buckled Layla in her booster seat. Layla yawned and wrapped her arms around Jessie as she reached over her.

"I'm tired, Mommy."

She squeezed back, thankful that one of her two children still gave spontaneous hugs. Her babies had grown up before she was ready. "We'll be home soon, and you can go to bed."

"Will you carry me?"

Layla was too big to be carried, but Jessie wouldn't pass up a chance to hold her close. "If you're asleep I will, sweetie." As soon as the answer left her mouth she knew she'd have a sleeping child whether by innocence or playing possum.

Corbin stood beside her open driver's door. "Since you'll already be working at the shelter, want me to pick up the kids after school and bring them over with me?"

"Um … yeah." Though he often had spurts of thoughtfulness, they never ceased to surprise her. Jessie touched the top of the door, her hand inches from his. "Thanks for thinking of it."

"Come on, Mom, I'm cold," Timmy pleaded from the back seat.

She hesitated a moment longer before climbing behind the wheel and starting the engine. Corbin shut the door. No "good-night, Jess." No peck on the cheek. In fact, he hadn't so much as touched her. Odd behavior from a man having just proposed.

***

"I'm getting married." Corbin spoke as he looked over the tightly scheduled calendar. "Guess

21

we'll have to fit it in on a weekend, maybe even a Sunday."

He and Jessie could empty her house over the Thanksgiving holiday and marry that Sunday. "Think you could help us move during break?"

"You're what?" Brock Warner's deep voice filled the tiny trailer.

Corbin turned to his lead worker and glanced up at the taller man. "That's what I said. Jessie's about to lose her house, and there's no sense in her moving to town and struggling to make ends meet."

"How—" Brock scratched his dark, bald head. "I thought you two fought as much as got along."

"No, not really. She's a bit of a spit-fire, but you just have to know how to take her." Corbin ignored Brock's widened eyes and moved to business. "We're close to falling behind schedule with the extended parking add-on. Let's see if we can't wrap up the west-wing of this plaza by the end of the week. That should keep us on target."

"When did she agree to this?" Brock followed him outside, completely unfocused on their current task. "You have asked her, right?"

"Of course I asked her."

"And she said yes?"

Corbin stopped short and repositioned his hat. "More or less. I'm talking with her again tonight. Yesterday was too busy. Now focus. We've a job to finish."

He'd expected Brock to respond with a slap on the back. He knew all about Jessie from the numerous stories Corbin shared. Corbin and Jessie had known each other for years and understood the other's personalities, their kids loved each other, and most of all Jessie wouldn't have to struggle anymore.

"I got the guys started." A couple minutes later, Brock reappeared at his side. "How long has this been going on?"

Corbin scrunched his brow. "Not every couple has a dating relationship before marriage, Brock."

"Uh huh, name one." He thunked Corbin's hardhat before walking away.

Chapter Three

Jessie tightened her robe around her worn flannel pajamas and waved to the children as they climbed the school bus steps. She closed the door and stared at the smudged fingerprints left in the paint more than a year before by Timmy. Soon she'd be sending her kids off from a different house, onto a different bus.

God, what am I to do?

The few apartments she'd checked into cost almost as much as her monthly house payment. And her electric company wasn't the same one that serviced town, which meant higher rates and a bigger bill. She could barely pay the one she received now. There wasn't any way she could afford to pay more.

Her mother had faced similar issues, and life hadn't proven any easier with age. She currently lived in a one bedroom apartment near senior citizen housing where she managed the social activities for the ninety-plus community. Obviously, living with her wasn't an option.

Jessie turned and dropped to her knees in front of the couch. With her arms on the cushion she buried her head in her hands. "Speak to me, God. Tell me what I should do."

"Fear not; I will help thee."

"For I know the thoughts that I think toward you ... thoughts of peace, and not of evil ..."

"Peace I leave with you, my peace I give unto you ... Let not your heart be troubled, neither let it be afraid."

Verse after verse flooded her mind in unmistakable clarity. She'd never been aware of God answering her this quickly. Jessie stood and paced the room while rubbing a knot at the base of her head.

"... for thou shalt not be ashamed: neither be thou confounded ... and shalt not remember the reproach of thy widowhood anymore."

She froze and a chill raced up her spine. That couldn't be a real verse. She reached for her Bible beside the table. What was God talking about?

In the back, she found the unnerving word, widow, followed by a list of verses locating its uses. She flipped to Isaiah 54 and scanned the first half of the chapter. "Lord, You're talking to Israel here, not me."

The verses came again, quieting her soul. God was communing with her in a voice she would recognize. His Word.

Jessie took a deep breath. "If this is Your will," she chewed her lip, "then I won't fight it." She held her breath, hoping to be given another option. None came.

Maybe I didn't hear Him right. Maybe this was just my mind making up possibilities. Even as she searched for other explanations, part of the Pastor's sermon came back to her. Something about heeding the voice of God and the consequences of not listening.

Okay. Fine. She took a deep breath. *So what's the next step?*

Corbin. Her stomach clenched at the thought of telling him. Even more at the thought of being married to a man who had yet to show any sign of affection. But if this was God's will, who was she to argue? She pressed her lips together in an effort not to answer her own question.

In her bedroom, Jessie picked up a brush and stared at the mirror as she combed her hair. Tears sprang to her eyes, not so much from the tangles the bristles caught as from pity for herself. Being married to a man who showed little or no emotion would be as awkward as a never-ending blind date.

Static raised her hair to stand on end. Great. The morning was even starting out like a blind date.

Half an hour later, with her mass of hair dampened and braided down her back, Jessie arrived at the shelter with a change of clothes in the seat beside her. She hoped to finish painting the new partition tonight to ready the rooms for anyone in need.

She stepped from her vehicle surprised to feel moisture in the air and glanced up. If the dull sky was any indication, she'd get a break from the woes of static. She grabbed her things from the van then entered the back of the shelter. The pastor's wife already had the back door unlocked and stood in the kitchen cracking eggs in a bowl.

"Hi, Vera." In her early forties, Vera possessed more spiritual wisdom than any woman Jessie had ever met.

Jessie plopped her bag onto the counter and reached for an apron. Made by an elderly member of their church, the fifties' style patterns always brought a smile to her face. Today, she chose the one embellished with cherries.

"Wade told me the good news." Vera smiled as she effortlessly whipped the eggs.

Jessie nodded and blinked back an instant response of tears. She licked her lips, delaying how to go about asking advice. Vera watched her closely.

"I am going to marry him." There. She'd said that much. Now moving on to the real issue. "But how do I deal with his—" The back door opened as her question finished silently in her mind ... *lack of affection?*

The other Thursday volunteers from church, Daisy, Oscar, Bobby Joe and Marilyn, filed in to join lunch preparations. Pastor Wade had masterminded the whole affair, stating their church had all the volunteers needed to make an impossible situation more bearable. Since then, whether small or large, a group of volunteers arrived at the shelter every Monday through Friday to prepare a meal for their area's increasing amount of homeless.

"What are we cooking today?" Bobby Joe reached for the menu and nodded his head in approval. "I like chicken and dumplings."

"And no one makes them better than you!" Vera turned as she spoke and poured the well-beaten eggs into the already prepared skillet. They sizzled over the hot pan drawing the attention of everyone in the room.

They were soon immersed in beginning preparations, all the while anticipating Vera's announcement of breakfast. It had become their Thursday ritual to start the day with a healthy dose of protein to get them through the hours of serving.

Bobby Joe prepared a large pot of water for boiling the chickens, while a husband and wife team, Daisy and Oscar, chopped vegetables for salad. Jessie watched the couple work in sync with the other as they washed and chopped, filling the bottom of a bowl with carrots, celery and pecans.

Jessie measured flour and sugar into a bowl. Sugar cookies were always a good hit, especially with those who had little teeth left to eat with. The counter mixer whirred with the determination of a jet fighter. It was no wonder someone had donated the old thing. She couldn't imagine having to use something like this every day in her home.

Someone tapped her shoulder causing her to jump.

"Time to eat." Daisy turned back to the table centered in the kitchen and took her usual seat beside Oscar.

Marilyn passed out the plates then her husband led the prayer.

Jessie watched the couples interact as she ate in silence. Oscar leaned over and stole a piece of bacon from Daisy's eggs.

Daisy playfully slapped his hand. "Now, Oscar, you stop that."

Their playful banter started up as usual, amusing the rest of the table. Had they always had this type of comradery or had it come about from years of relying on each other? She turned her focus to the other couple. Though they didn't often tease, there was an unmistakable comfort that came from years of trust. Would she and Corbin ever have that?

The morning sped toward lunch and soon, the cookie scented air was thick with expectancy as familiar faces lined up to accept a hot meal. Jessie greeted each one. Many she knew by name, others she still had to learn.

"Hey, Jessie-girl." Nevin, a disabled veteran, waved to her from his usual seat.

Jessie grabbed her bag and left the kitchen. She greeted the wiry gray-haired man by draping an arm across his scratchy wool, covered shoulders and hugging him tight. "How are you today? Did they put enough on your plate?"

Nevin snuck a look toward the kitchen. "I wouldn't mind another cookie if there's any left over."

"No need." She reached into her bag. "I brought you some from home."

Nevin accepted the small bag of chocolate chip cookies, his favorite. His eyes watered as he laughed. "You're spoiling me."

"You're worth spoiling."

Jessie moved on to give him a moment to collect himself. Nevin was still coming to terms with the recent changes in his life, and his emotions were often near the surface. As part of a program from a city shelter their church cooperated with, good conduct had earned him a chance to move here where they helped secure him a small home and a part time job. Nevin's disabilities limited labor potential, but not his spirit. Always jovial and optimistic, he was often the first to lend a helping hand with new members in the shelter. His compassion for others had woven a path into Jessie's heart. Even her children were always excited to see him.

After wiping down a table, Jessie returned and pulled out a chair across from him. Her job at the shelter didn't end with serving food, but connecting with as many as she could. "Have you heard from your daughter lately?"

Nevin took a napkin and wiped cookie crumbs from his beard. "Yes. She got hired at that fancy vet office I told you about. I guess she's one of the owners or partners now or something like that."

"That's great news."

From stories he'd shared, Nevin returned from the war and became a wealthy businessman. But continued pressure for success coupled with posttraumatic stress, Nevin lost his energy and drive. Then his family and career. No longer hopeful, he took to living on the streets.

"Yeah, her mama did a fine job of raising her."

"And no doubt, your training in her early life had something to do with it, too." Jessie squeezed his hand.

"Nah, I don't deserve any credit, and that doesn't bother me. I'm just thankful for her success and pray for her continued happiness."

As always, Jessie swallowed down other questions that loomed in her mind. Did his daughter ever visit? Didn't they want to see each other? But it wasn't her business or her place to ask.

Jessie made her way to visit others before those who'd arrived by bus had to leave. It wasn't until she started to clean the kitchen that she noticed a new family huddled near the door. The mother's timid face took in the interior of the room. Her eyes seemed hungry, not for food, but for something to hope in. Jessie nudged Vera, "How much do we have left?"

Vera set down the pot she'd removed from the counter and glanced over her shoulder at the family of six. "Enough."

Jessie looked in the pot. There didn't seem enough to feed two people, much less six. But God had performed greater miracles than this numerous times in the Bible. She was sure He could handle this small need. Instinctively, they bowed their heads and said a prayer over the food.

Jessie moved to the dining room. "Please come in and take a seat. We'll bring you something to eat."

The eldest of the five boys encamped around their mother couldn't have been older than her and Corbin's sons. He worked his mouth in worry, while his younger brothers smiled and sniffed the air as if eager to fill their bellies.

After shuffling through the refrigerator, they found left over rolls from earlier in the week and cleaned carrots. By adding them to each plate, there was plenty of food. *Thank you, God.*

Leaving the family to eat in peace, Jessie resumed her task of cleaning. Bob and Marilyn had already done a good share of the work before they left. Oscar stayed in the dining room, drawing laughter from the boys.

Vera drew to her side. "Did you want to finish what you started earlier?"

Oh, yes, she certainly did, but not with so many chances for interruption. "Maybe later. I think we're still too busy for conversation."

Vera nodded in understanding. "I'll keep praying for you." Her statement wasn't made lightly. Vera's prayers were full of enough wisdom and heartfelt need they would rival a saint.

Daisy draped her cleaning cloth over the handle of the oven. "All the tables are clean except for the one still in use." She tapped her fingers over the rings on her left hand, a habit she had when something was on her mind. "I heard the young woman mention they were living in a motel. I can't imagine how they're making ends meet."

They're not. Jessie watched the boys interacting with Oscar. One climbed on his lap and pulled his ear lobe. "Why are your ears so long?" She stifled a giggle as she caught the look of embarrassment from his mother. The woman said something Jessie couldn't hear before gathering the empty bowls and bringing them to the kitchen.

"Thank you, so much. The food was delicious."

Jessie took the dishes and handed them to Vera before focusing on the young mother. "You're welcome. By the way, I'm Jessie."

"My name's Heather."

Although Jessie had heard Daisy's comment of how they lived, she used the subject as a lead-in to learn if there was another way they could help. "Do you have a place to stay?"

One of the younger sons turned and announced, "We live in a hotel!"

"Motel, silly," the eldest corrected.

Heather's gaze studied the counter which separated her from Jessie. "It's just 'til we get back on our feet."

The woman didn't look like she lived a rough life. As always, Jessie, wondered at the events that led to their homelessness. Not everyone could be saved, this she realized. Some wouldn't manage no matter how much was given them. But there were others, like Nevin, who just needed a little support to get them back to being self-sufficient.

Jessie studied the boys and their growing rowdiness. "How do you do it? With all boys." Shame for asking heated her face. Experience had taught her you do what you have to do to get by. "I'm sorry. It's just that my two boys are so rambunctious."

"That's okay. I appreciate the sympathy." She gave a short laugh. "Sometimes a friend helps out. And we try to go to the park a lot after school. The oldest aren't there today because they had slight fevers when they woke up. I thought the hot lunch might help them get over it quicker."

Jessie sucked her bottom lip between her teeth. If they were sick, the chilly weather wouldn't help. "Did you walk?"

"Yeah."

"An' it was cold!" The same hyper boy added.

Heather's gaze again dropped as she concentrated on wiping her toddler's face.

Jessie couldn't let them walk. With her mind made up, she said, "Let me get some cookies for your boys to take with them and then you can ride home in my van."

She knew not to word it as a question or the woman would likely turn her down to save pride.

The women in the kitchen turned questioning glances her direction. Vera met her as she bagged the cookies. "I understand you wanting to help, but we know nothing about them. I can't let you go alone. I'll go with you."

Vera's protectiveness came as no surprise. They'd been warned of the dangers they could face when starting the shelter. Still, Jessie felt it was the right thing to do. "You can't. There won't be enough seats."

Chapter Four

Jessie pulled into the oldest and cheapest motel in town. The single story building ran the length of half a block with veneer-peeled doors facing the street. A couple of men, smoking cigarettes, loitered outside of one of the rooms. Further down sat another man on an upturned crate with his head in his hands. "Do you feel safe here?"

Heather kept her somber gaze forward. "No. But it's better than living on the streets." Her wedding ring caught the reflection of the afternoon sun as she brushed a lock of hair from her eyes.

Several families had moved to the area after the new prison was built to be closer to their incarcerated loved ones. Was this her story? Since none of the kids were in a hurry to leave the van, Jessie pointed to the ring on the woman's left hand. "Are you married?"

"Yes, and my husband's a good man." She studied Jessie before continuing. "A lot of people on the streets aren't there because of alcoholism or drug abuse."

"I know that."

Disbelief flashed across Heather's eyes.

An urge to gain her trust pressed Jessie to admit why. "I've been there."

***

Jessie's cell phone rang as Heather slid the door shut on the van. After waving good-bye, she looked at the caller and answered. "I'm fine, Vera."

Their conversation went on for another few minutes before she reminded Vera not to lock the shelter. "I'm coming back to paint."

"Alone?" Vera sighed. "Jessie, I'm glad you're marrying Corbin. Then he can take over worrying about that too-trusting nature of yours."

"Speaking of which, there's no need to worry, he'll be there soon with the kids." Mist covered the windshield like delicate muslin. Jessie turned onto the road then flipped the wiper blades on low to clear the spray caused from other vehicles.

She said good-bye and drove on deep in thought. Vera's concern was warranted. As a pastor's wife, she often saw people take advantage of the church. She didn't want the same thing to happen to Jessie. But her comment about Corbin was the real thorn to Jessie. There was no doubt Corbin would worry over her, but it was the thoughtless way he'd go about it that caused her stomach to knot.

At the shelter, Jessie changed into stained overalls. Among the many colors of splattered dry paint was the pink she used in Layla's room, the green from Timmy's and the deep purple her husband had so disliked in their bedroom. She'd planned to change it and had even bought a neutral eggshell color, only he'd died before she could. Now the color was in the shelter's kitchen. It was just as well she hadn't changed her bedroom, the forthcoming new owners loved the walls.

Jessie laid a sheet of plastic over the floor before filling her roller pan. After trimming out the wall with a small brush and a step ladder, she looked for the extension to her hand roller. A thorough search of the shelter proved it wasn't there. Either she'd left it at home or someone had more need of it than her. No biggie, she'd rely on the ladder for the high areas.

She returned to her paint and roller as the back door creaked open. Jessie's heart lodged in her throat. Vera's concerns now amplified as she remembered not locking the door. Maybe someone thought the shelter was still serving lunch?

"We're not open right now." Jessie called to what she hoped was no one. She glanced at her watch. Four in the afternoon.

A chill raced up her spine. Most of the people they fed seemed harmless, but there were always the few that looked as though they lived a life of crime. Jessie didn't want to pass judgment—everyone had a past—but the vibes they sent off always left her unnerved.

She glanced around for what she could use for defense. Other than the ladder, there wasn't anything in the room, and unlike Jacki Chan, she'd probably entangle the rungs around her neck.

Her heart beat faster as the voices drew near. Then she recognized them. "Hi kids." Her voice came out a little too relieved. "I'm back here."

"Mom!" Layla ran into the room and paused as she took in the paint and ladder. "Can I paint, too?"

"No, you little munchkin." Corbin swung her up and tickled her ribs. "You get to play games like the other kids."

Aside from her foolish imagination, Jessie battled an onslaught of feelings. How could she describe the emotions that rose as Corbin entered? Relief. Gladness. And something else. Something she wasn't sure she wanted to credit toward her often male chauvinistic neighbor.

The smile he cast her way held uncertainty. Was he still serious about the proposal or was he wondering how to back out?

"Thanks for getting the kids." She glanced at her watch. "I brought some cookies as an after-school snack. That should hold them until dinner."

"Okay." Corbin checked out the room. What would he find wrong? To her surprise he turned to leave.

"You're leaving footprints." She pointed to where he'd been standing.

"Yeah, that happens when it rains."

Jessie narrowed her eyes. "Don't you think you should take off your shoes so you don't track up the floor?"

"Nope." He knocked his toe against the door frame. "These are steel-toed. They protect my feet."

"That's not really a problem, is it? You're just fixing a spot in the floor not building a mall."

Corbin smiled at her remark before leaving her to paint. He seemed to enjoy their quibbles as much as they annoyed her. Jessie slid the roller into the paint. She'd poured more than intended. Paint oozed over the end caps of the foam cylinder.

Thankfully, she'd prepared for this by laying plastic over the entire floor.

Reaching on tiptoe, she strained to paint the corner. Though she could easily move her ladder she didn't want to take the time for such a small area. Concentrating on her balance and the wall, the roller connected with the strip of paint left earlier by her brush.

"I'm going to—"

Startled by Corbin's sudden reappearance, she jerked to the side, her back tightened and one arm flung in the air. The ladder rocked on its feet. Corbin raced forward and grabbed her waist as something slapped against the corner of the pan. Huge globs of white paint flew into the air. Corbin sidestepped but didn't release his hold. The ladder rocked again, as he pulled her weight to the side.

"Let go!" Jessie's cry came a second too late. She lost her hold and fell against Corbin. The wet roller slipped from her hand as she blocked the fall of the ladder with her arm. Corbin stumbled backward then lost his footing, and they both crumpled to the floor.

"What were you doing?" They spoke simultaneously.

"Ooh," Jessie looked back to see her hand smashed against the wet foam roller. She moved her legs off Corbin and burst out laughing. "Look at your jeans!" Splatters of white raced up his calf and thigh. She laughed even more. "You stepped in the pan."

"Very funny. I wouldn't have if you hadn't been falling."

"You snuck up on me while I was painting."

They both stood, staring accusingly at one another, yet with enough amusement to keep from getting mad. Then Corbin looked at the bottom of his shoes. "Great. I slipped on your roller. Now I can't wear my boots."

"Sorry." A smile she couldn't hide, stretched across Jessie's mouth.

"Yeah, me too."

"Thanks for catching me."

"Again."

"Humph. You don't have to bring last week into this."

Why didn't he respond? Jessie looked up. Corbin stared at her with a curious expression. His chest rose and fell with a sigh before he stated, "Be careful on there," referring to the ladder.

As he bent to unlace his boots, he added, "I came back in to tell you I'm going to hang a sheet of plastic over the door so any sawdust I create won't stick to your wall."

"Good idea."

Corbin left his boots by the plastic door he'd created and Jessie resumed her job. It took several swipes to free the smashed fibers in the brush, but nothing seemed to help the side of the roller that was now caved in from Corbin's boot. The roller continued to skip from the dent, making her work twice as hard to cover the wall.

Jessie smiled despite the extra aggravation. This time Corbin's helpfulness had been the cause of the mishap—not her. Though sure he wouldn't see it as such, Jessie gained a certain amount of satisfaction knowing it wasn't always her making mistakes.

"Owww!" Corbin yelled from the other room. "What in the—"

Jessie scrambled down the ladder and to the opposite side of the shelter. She poked her head in the doorway as their children crowded around her. "What's wrong?"

Corbin hopped on one foot, his face twisted in pain. "Who decided to use the plywood as a chalkboard?"

"Me-eee!" Layla gleefully raised her hand and mimicked Corbin's hopping.

The full sheet of wood now laid haphazardly on top of other pieces of cut lumber. One end completely covered in an elementary copy of the magical flower in her daughter's favorite Disney film.

"What happened?" Jessie glanced back to Corbin's sock covered foot he now hobbled on as he righted the board.

He grimaced, "My hand slipped on the chalk and I dropped the board on my toe."

Was she missing something? It didn't seem like he should be in that much pain. Hadn't it just fallen over on its side? "That's all?"

"Yep," his jaw tightened, "*that's all.*"

"Dad, you were jumping like a kangaroo!" Garret's infectious laughter had a rippling effect on the rest of the kids.

Jessie fought the temptation to follow suit. Usually tough as nails, seeing Corbin upset over something as small as his toe somehow seemed extra comedic, still she didn't like seeing him in pain. "Guess you should've left your boots on, huh?"

Although she spoke the thought with sincerity, Corbin didn't seem to take it as such. A tendon bulged in his jaw as he shook his head.

Maybe tonight wasn't the right time to answer his question about marriage.

***

Corbin guided everyone through the door of the local Italian restaurant. A simple burger joint would have been more suited for his paint stained attire, but the children had rallied against him. Though now, he was beginning to regret his soft-hearted decision. Their two hour wait at the shelter had caused far too much energy. "*Garret.*" He called his son away from the display of desserts as they followed the hostess to their table then almost tripped over Layla twirling in front of him.

"Tracey will be your server tonight." The hostess passed out their menus. "She'll be right with you."

Moments later a young college-aged girl bounced to their table.

"Hi, I'm Tracey with an 'e-y' not a plain ole' 'y'," she bobbed her head between each shoulder, "and I'll be your waitress this evening."

Corbin chanced a peek at Jessie. Did she find Tracey with an "e-y" as annoying as he did? An enlarged vein visibly thrummed in her temple. He bit back a laugh and returned his attention to their waitress.

"Oh, you are so cute," Tracey bent toward Layla, "and I just love the way your bright socks don't match anything you're wearing ..." Their waitress shared her enthusiasm with each member of the family, smiling so much her eyes became curved slits.

When at last their orders were taken and Tracey had gone, Corbin sighed heavily. "I think our waitress escaped from a happiness cult."

Jessie's laughter tumbled out with the ease he'd hoped to see tonight. Nothing at the shelter had gone right, at least not for him, and he feared they'd never get a chance to talk about the proposal.

He relaxed with her, enjoying the sight of her pretty smile. "Do you realize this is the first time we've gone out together?"

Her smile faltered and he quickly stated, "I mean all of us ... as a family." Ugh, he still wasn't saying things right. "I mean—"

"It's okay," her hand briefly touched his, "I know what you mean."

Then was she ready to talk about—

"Okay, Mr. Freckles had the Dr. Pepper ..." The cult lady had returned. She passed Timmy his drink then continued with nicknames for the rest of the children. Her head bobbed uncontrollably again as she asked, "Have you decided what you want?"

Was the whole "I'm the friendliest waitress in the world" thing an act or was she seriously cursed as a child? Corbin didn't know, but he'd gladly give her an enormous tip to leave their table for the rest of the evening.

"Ahem." Jessie made a slight motion with her finger over her mouth then drew her brows together.

He was scowling and hadn't realized it. Forcing his brows upward to erase the evidence of Tracey's effect, Corbin cleared his throat and recited their list of orders.

"Okey-dokey, we'll get those done and not be pokey!"

As soon as she left, Jessie snorted with pent up laughter. "Your expression was priceless."

"What expression? You mean this one?" Feeling playful, he put on a silly smile then poked Shannon seated next to him. "Okey-dokey, pokey."

She squirmed and rolled her eyes.

His pre-teenager found Dad's silly antics in public, embarrassing.

"I can make her laugh." Garret reached across the table to aggravate his sister.

"Garret—no!"

His son's elbow bumped against Timmy's soda knocking it on its side and splashing into Corbin's lap. Corbin clenched his jaw as the remaining dark, syrupy liquid oozed across the table in a thinning branch. His jeans were drenched—across both thighs.

Silence enveloped the table as the glass continued to rock back and forth, sloshing out the last of the soda. Corbin inhaled deeply, kept his face expressionless, and looked across at Jessie. "As you were saying."

Her eyes lit with humor as she covered her mouth. A blush rose to her cheeks from holding her response in check. "I have a bag of donated clothes from church in the car that I forgot to drop off at the shelter. I'll see what I can find for you."

He leaned back in his chair as the children watched in interest. "No hurry. I'm not going anywhere."

After Jessie left, Garret finally spoke. "I'm sorry, Dad."

"That's okay. It happens, just hopefully not too often."

A moment later Jessie returned, pulling her mouth to the side while averting her eyes. "This is all I could find that would fit you."

He stared at the item hanging from her hand. "You expect me to wear pink shorts?"

Her wide smile showed off her perfectly straight teeth. "If you don't want to remain sticky."

A woman seated across from them rose her brows in sympathy.

"Dad, you can't be serious." Shannon sank down in her seat. "Everyone will see you."

Corbin yanked the shorts from Jessie's hand. "You're enjoying this evening way too much." He tried for a sour look before limping toward the restroom. First his toe, now his pride. What else did he have to lose?

After changing, he rolled up his jeans and stopped in front of the mirror. If ever there was a time in his life he wanted an escape, now was that time.

He could do this. Construction workers were tough. He would walk out there as though nothing was out of the ordinary and enjoy his dinner.

His expression stared back at him, and he felt sorry for the guy in the mirror. Well, almost. He knew before he proposed, that life with Jessie would bring plenty of adventure. *So toughen up, if she says yes, this is just the beginning.* He caught the wry smile in the mirror before turning to leave.

Weaving through the tables of other diners, his ears burned from subtle laughter left in his wake. If only he could trade them places.

A mocking hoot tumbled loudly from his son as he neared the table. Garret held his side and pointed at his dad. "There's another color for the rainbow, Layla."

Layla frowned. "Them's not red. Him's wearing pink shorts."

And thank you for that public announcement.

"They're and he." Jessie corrected.

"They … I mean, he's got pink."

Jessie had been correcting her daughter's speech for the last two years. She'd mentioned hoping school would fix the problem. So far it hadn't.

"Dad, you're so embarrassing." Shannon pulled her side swept bangs back to the middle of her forehead and covered her eyes. "And Layla, just ask Jessie. She'll know all the colors of the rainbow."

He took his seat as Jessie continued the conversation he'd missed while changing. She said, "Roy G. Biv."

"What?" The resounding question drew a quiet pause at their table.

"Red, orange, yellow, green, blue, indigo and violet. The initials spell out the name, Roy G. Biv. Now you try it." While the kids tried to memorize the colors and spot them in the room, Jessie turned to Corbin with mischief in her eyes. "Nice legs."

The heat of embarrassment climbed his neck with a searing warmth. How did anyone with a large family ever manage to eat out?

Chapter Five

With the fiasco they called dinner over, Corbin escorted everyone outside with his sticky jeans rolled beneath his arm. The hostess hurried to open the door as though eager for them to leave. Her mouth moved silently as the kids walked past. Was she counting to make sure they didn't leave any behind?

With the thought in mind, Corbin also counted to ensure they were all still with him then glanced at Jessie. Her hands were shoved deep in her pockets for warmth. Just as well, he wasn't much of a hand holder anyway. Would she expect that type of relationship? He thought back to when her husband had been alive. He couldn't recall them holding hands.

Jessie's long dark hair bounced against her back as her gait quickened to keep up with his. He slowed his steps. No need to hurry the evening along when it just became enjoyable.

Jessie had said nothing about marrying him. But thanks to Shannon's announcement to the woman at church, she had to have given it thought. Why hadn't she brought it up, or was she waiting on him?

"Mom," Timmy gained his and Jessie's attention. "Garret said we get to live with him when you marry Corbin. I can't wait! I'm gonna sleep in the top of my bunk like Garret does and we can have nerf gun wars!"

"Yeah!" Garret responded, adding to Timmy's enthusiasm.

Before Corbin could gauge Jessie's response, Layla left Shannon's side and raced toward them. "Will, will—" She tripped and her hands flew forward catching on Corbin's shorts.

Pop!

The last of the rotten elastic band's strength gave way.

Corbin caught Layla's wrist before she hit the pavement, but his shorts had already reached his knees. Laughter erupted from the boys and even Shannon, as cold November wind heckled against his bare legs.

He hauled Layla up then calmly reached for his shorts. He'd given the evening too much credit. With four children, enjoyment was more of a moment by moment experience.

Between giggles, Jessie managed to clear her throat. "Um, nice legs … and backside."

Corbin pulled up his shorts and heaved a massive sigh. The best thing to do was continue as though nothing had happened. Which of course would be a lot easier if the comedic bunch accompanying him could control their humor.

"I'm t'orry." Layla, his only supporter, apologized.

"Not a problem." He patted her shoulder while his other hand clung to the offending shorts.

"Me, too, for laughing," Jessie spoke around a smile that wouldn't fade. "And I do admire your patience."

"Co'bin," Layla pulled at his sleeve, "are you goin' be my daddy?"

"I'm planning on it."

"You still want to?" Jessie's brows arched upward. "After tonight?"

"Your stalling is the only thing testing my patience." If she wanted his help, she needed to make a decision now. They wouldn't have much time to move everything from her house otherwise. "What's your answer, Jess? And please hurry. I'm starting to lose feeling in my legs."

Her grin broadened as her laughing eyes took in his pitiful situation. "Yes."

***

Jessie taped the bottom of another box and emptied the shelf of books beside the couch as last night played through her mind. Corbin had displayed more patience than any man she knew. Never once, did he say anything hurtful or raise his voice. Not even her late husband could have managed the whole day's events with that much grace.

She considered Corbin's response to her answer of marriage.

"You've prayed about it?" His probing request said a lot. He didn't want her entering the marriage on blind faith.

"I did."

Relief seemed to course through him as he'd sighed and momentarily closed his eyes. Was it that important she marry him? The romantic side of her wished it was because of love, that he couldn't live without her, but she knew better. Corbin was as practical as they came. The duteous side of him could now relax as he'd kept a family off the streets, or at least from living in poverty. The other side of him could cheer because he didn't have to search for a new babysitter.

Now she was being snide.

Forgive me, God.

Did it really matter what reason he had for marriage since God Himself assured her it was to be? She tucked her cheek against her shoulder. Yes, it mattered. Whether it should or not, it did.

God, please let him love me.

***

Through the window, Jessie watched the children hop off the bus and run to the door. Once inside, Timmy tossed his backpack on the floor. "What can I box up, Mom?"

"You can start by picking that up," she pointed to his bag, "then clean your room. The things you don't want we'll donate to the shelter." *At least what he hasn't already broken.*

"Oh, here's the mail." He handed her a single pink envelope. "Is it from Grandma?"

Jessie nodded. Though a week late, her mother had remembered her birthday. She slid her finger beneath the envelope's flap and removed the card. A woman in a green dress with her hair styled in a retro fashion held a martini in her hand. Her bright red lips frozen in a sly smile.

"What's it say? What's it say?" The children crowded to see.

Jessie peeked inside and read the punch line to herself then held the card flat against her chest. "You know Grandma's a little rough around the edges, so you don't need to read this one." Her mother's humor wasn't always fit for the children, but Jessie didn't hold it against her. She hadn't been left holding a week old baby to raise by herself. Nor had she had to scrape by to make ends meet only to live in the worst side of town.

Timmy snickered and ran off with Garret, while Shannon's curious gaze followed her to the kitchen.

"Won't she be our grandma, too?"

"I'm hungry." Layla opened the refrigerator.

"You're interrupting. Sit down and I'll get you some Jello." Jessie finished addressing her youngest then turned to Shannon. "Yes, she'll be your grandma, too."

"Then what do you mean by rough?"

She cringed. There was a big difference between her mother and Corbin's parents. Jessie had met Corbin's parents. They traveled up from Texas several times a year and always made a point to visit with Jessie and the kids. They were kind, gentle, and loving. Shannon and Garret often received gifts from them, and while Grandma baked, Grandpa played.

Samantha, Jessie's mom, on the other hand, didn't visit often, didn't call often, and didn't buy gifts. Instead, she expected her daughter to do those things while she lived it up at the retirement community center. Samantha not only scheduled and planned their activities, but joined in as well. Still, Jessie was happy for her mother. After a life of rejection and disappointment, she finally seemed happy.

She considered how to answer Shannon. "You know how some of the people that eat at the shelter are a little rough? Well, my mother didn't have an easy life and in a small way, is a little bit like that."

Compassion softened Shannon's features. The girl had a heart of gold. "Is she happy she'll have more grandkids?"

Jessie bit her lip. "I haven't told her yet."

Shannon nodded in silent consideration before leaving the room to do her homework. Left alone, Jessie prepared an easy dish of baked garlic chicken with potatoes and apples. By the time the work had been accomplished she could no longer avoid her conscience. She dialed her mother's work number.

"Mom?"

"Hi, honey." Familiar with her mother's habits, Jessie could picture her taking a drag from her cigarette during the slight pause. When her coarse voice returned, it was to tell whom she danced with last night at the festivity she'd planned.

With the phone pressed against her ear, Jessie rested her elbow on the wall and rubbed her temple with her other hand. "Mom," Jessie cut in. If she didn't tell her now, she might lose her nerve. "I'm sorry to interrupt, but I called to tell you I'm getting married."

The sudden silence was finally broken with one word. "Why?"

Jessie swallowed past a lump in her throat. Her mother, thrilled that Jessie had met a man who was honest and dependable, had loved Richard like her own son. His death had rocked her as much as Jessie. Was she against him being replaced?

"Because it makes sense. The kids are young. They need a dad." She closed her eyes. *That was the reason?* Her pathetic answer grated against her ears.

"Who is he?"

"Corbin Vaughn."

"Your neighbor?" A sharp laugh followed. "I should've seen that one coming."

"What?"

"Never mind. If he makes you happy, then I'm happy for you." The sound of her blowing smoke through her lips whispered across the line. "Are the kids excited?"

"Yes."

"Well, Baby, it's better than scraping by. I just hope it works."

Not long after Jessie hung up Corbin appeared, ready to sort through her bills as they had planned.

He stood at the table without pulling out a chair. "What's wrong?"

Was she that transparent? Like waiting for an x-ray with a lead blanket on her chest, she struggled to pull in a deep breath. "Are we doing the right thing?" Part of her hadn't wanted to ask, in fear he'd back out and she'd be left wondering where to go.

He clasped her upper arm. "Of course we are."

His eyes held a gentle understanding, at least that's what Jessie wanted them to read. She glanced at his hand. He actually touched her ... and her skin flamed from the contact.

"Who did you talk to today?"

She looked away. He was far too perceptive. "My mother."

"That explains it."

She frowned. "What does that mean? You haven't even met her." Although they only lived twenty miles apart, her mother rarely drove the distance to Jessie's house.

"Doesn't Samantha work for the retirement community in town?" He continued after her nod. "My crew and I built their additional housing units."

"How did you know she was my mother?"

He pointed to a framed photograph of Grandma and the kids. Something akin to panic rose inside. She ran through her mother's response on the phone. What did she mean she should've seen it coming? Had Corbin talked about her?

"Let's get to the bills." Corbin's stomach growled as he sat down. He smiled sheepishly and shrugged. "Dinner smells good."

Jessie marveled at the way his visage could change from task-driven, hard-working man, to boyhood charm. She cleared her throat and searched for a distraction. She grabbed the file box from off the floor. If things didn't slow down, her carousel of feelings would make her sick.

They settled into the task of sorting out the business side of marriage. Embarrassed by her state of affairs, her stomach tightened as she withdrew the last bill statement. "And there you have it."

Without a trace of cynicism, Corbin looked over the papers. "Do the new owners want the appliances?"

"All but the stove."

"One of my guys might want that." He tapped on the calculator then looked beside him at Jessie. "This isn't as bad as you might have thought. If the new owners agree to the price, then you'll have enough to pay for the car repair, the fridge, and the cell phone bill. That just leaves the credit card for us to pay off."

Ugh. He'd already made known he didn't approve of the way she used her card. She prepared herself to receive a lecture. Then it donned on her what he'd said. "You don't mind? Paying for my bill?"

"Of course not. You'll be my wife." He tapped the papers with his finger. "I honestly don't know how you've made it this long. You should've said something. I would've paid you more."

Jessie's heart did a slow spin. There was more to this man than she'd let herself realize.

Later that evening, for the second night in a row, they sat down together as a family. Everyone bowed their heads for grace. A quiet strain pulled Jessie's attention back to Corbin. His look said he was waiting for her as it was her house. She asked, "Would you mind?"

"Certainly." Corbin bowed his head. "Thank you, Father, for bringing us together tonight." He paused, "And for uniting us as a family."

Jessie peeked from lowered lashes as Corbin glanced her way. She quickly dropped her head again, embarrassed she'd been caught.

Was he feeling any of the things she was? Confusion mainly. Of course it was ideal to be attracted to the one you were marrying, but did *he* feel anything? Oh, if only she knew.

After prayer, the family came alive with energy. Several children spoke at once.

Shannon passed the salad to Jessie. "Play practice starts next week. I'll have to stay late after school two days a week until the play."

"What days will that be?"

"I don't know."

Jessie hoped it didn't interfere with her schedule at the shelter. She enjoyed working with the same people each week.

Garret dropped his fork against his plate with a loud clang. "Don't tell them." His supposed whisper was loud enough for everyone to hear.

"Don't tell us what?" Corbin looked from his son to Timmy.

Timmy stared at his plate, refusing to talk.

Garret picked up his fork and shoved his food around. "I got sent to the office today."

"What for?" Corbin remained calm, clearly giving the boy a chance to explain himself.

"I punched Nick Stanley. But he punched me first!"

Jessie's eyes widened as she looked from son to father.

"He kicked me under the lunch table. I told him to quit and he did it again." He looked straight at his dad. "I did what you taught me. I'd asked him to stop and he didn't. So I warned him I'd get him back."

"And boy, did he!" Timmy interjected. "That 'ole Nick isn't too smart, cause he kicked Garret a third time and—"

"Timmy," Jessie interrupted. "Let Garret explain."

"Well, Son, what did you do?" Corbin took another bite as he calmly waited for Garret to finish explaining.

Garret shrugged. "I reached over the table and slugged him."

"Right in the nose!" Timmy's pride over Garret's actions worried Jessie. They'd never upheld any form of violence in their household.

"Sounds to me like you did the right thing. You asked him to stop first. Then told him what was going to happen. You can't help it if he didn't listen. Did the principle understand?"

"Yep." Garret pushed back from the table. "Nick gets in-school suspension and since this was his second offense, he'll get suspended next time."

Jessie's mind whirled. What had Corbin been talking about? He actually supported his son fighting? Boy, did they have a lot to learn about each other.

The children asked to be excused and left the table.

Not wanting to mess up the agreeable evening by bringing up their differences, Jessie switched topics. "I met a new family at the shelter yesterday."

Corbin reached for his glass but waited to drink until after Jessie explained.

"The mom is Heather, and she has five boys all under the age of seven."

His eyes followed the forms of their retreating sons. "You should put her on the prayer list."

Jessie smiled in agreement.

"Is there a dad in the picture?"

"Yes. His name is Dale and he works construction in the city. Their landlord sold the apartment building where they lived without telling any of the residents. Then one day a knock sounded on the door and they were evicted. The new owner said they'd had two months to move out. Only they didn't, because their landlord had chosen to keep collecting rent and not let anyone know."

Corbin's face puckered in a deep frown. "What'd they do?"

"They tried living with her mother, but that didn't work for long. Now they're staying in a motel."

"That can't be easy with five boys ... or practical. With the cost of a motel room, they'll never save enough to establish another rental." Corbin cleared his throat. "Too often, I think we're quick to judge people when really it could be us."

Was he thinking about her and how close she'd been to being in the same position before accepting his offer? She met his gaze. No. He saw the truth most people hid from. The only security in life was through Jesus Christ and trusting everything to Him. All else, history had proven, could be lost in a blink of an eye.

"I think Heather thought I'd judge her. But having been there, I can too easily relate."

"Been there? You mean if we *didn't* marry?"

"No." Jessie stacked the plates. "My mom lost her job when I was fifteen. Before she found another one, we lost our home."

"Where did you live?"

"In our car."

His face froze. Surprise and concern etched his features.

"It was only for a year and I took showers at school, so it wasn't as bad as it sounds."

He stared at his empty glass. Several moments passed before he spoke again. "Do you know where to find the family?"

"Yes. I drove them home."

With deliberate, slow movements, he moved his hands from the table to his lap and leaned back in his chair. "You drove them home? A family you've never met before?" A muscle bulged in his jaw. "Jessie, you've sat through the same training I did. Please tell me someone went with you."

The familiar feeling of child in trouble, weighed on her conscience. "There wasn't room in the van. But I—"

"You have children expecting their mother to be home when they're home, and you put your life at risk like that?" He raked a hand through his hair. When he spoke, his voice held a forced calm. "Don't do that again. Call me at work. I'll leave and follow you if I have to, but don't ever go alone."

"All right, but I knew she was okay. I had a feeling ..."

"Promise. Me." Worry or disappointment, she couldn't tell, forged deep lines around his eyes.

Chapter Six

Saturday morning came too early for Corbin. Unable to sleep, he woke before the sun and shuffled to the kitchen. He grabbed a cup from the cabinet and set it on the counter. The ceramic bottom made a loud clink against the tile. His ears shrunk toward his shoulders. No matter how hard he tried, he could never be quiet in the mornings. Though his kids were used to his habits and could sleep through anything, he didn't know how Timmy and Layla would respond.

A smile warmed his heart at the thought of adding two more children to his home. He loved Jessie's kids. Always had. After their father died, both children had grown more attached to him. Often joining his children in telling about their days whenever he stopped by to take Shannon and Garret home.

Jessie, he was certain, thought the same of his children. The marriage was a good idea. One that appealed to him more and more. He checked the time. Too early to call Pastor Wade, but before leaving to help pack, he'd place a call to reserve the date they'd agreed on last night.

The subject of the wedding always made Jessie blush. Corbin had wondered if she'd even discuss it with him. But in his first marriage, he learned the best time to hold a woman's attention was when helping clean the kitchen. So as she washed the dishes and he dried, he'd approached the subject.

"When do the new owners want to be in the house?"

"Before Christmas." A strand of hair caught on her thick lashes. With her hands in the soapy water, she'd blown it temporarily out of the way. "Actually, they want enough time to get settled in so they can have a big 'Christmas Show the House Off' party."

"I'd call the bank and get the closing date scheduled as soon as you can. Then we could marry the Sunday after Thanksgiving."

"In two weeks?" Her eyes widened.

"I'm on a tight schedule at work and with having to empty your house and the holiday coming up, I doubt we could do it sooner."

"No, no, that's fine," she'd stammered and blushed.

Looking back, Corbin was certain she would've liked to wait even longer, but they couldn't if she wanted a sure sale. Besides, they'd known one another long enough, there wasn't reason for a prolonged engagement.

Dressed in the insulated coveralls he wore to work, Corbin sipped his coffee and entered the garage. He stared at the boxes stacked in the corner. Beth's clothes. He'd never dropped them off, thinking he couldn't chance seeing someone else dressed like his wife.

Now four years later, it was time to let go. He loaded them into the bed of his truck, along with half used cans of paint, broken lawn chairs he'd never get around to fixing, and other assorted items he wouldn't miss. By the time he was done, half the garage stood open for storage. Once the kids woke up, he'd treat them to breakfast then stop at the local thrift store and the dump.

***

"Your fridge is as spotless as a new one." Corbin removed the jug of tea and shut the door.

"It's only three months old." Jessie filled their glasses and handed one to him.

"Mine wouldn't still look like this. When do you have time to clean it?"

Her shoulders slumped as she sighed. "At night. I can't sleep by myself. The bed's too big and empty."

Corbin watched her stare off into nothing. Her naturally dark, pink lips pulled to the side as she lost herself in private thoughts. If the empty bed was a problem, their marriage would fix that.

He continued to gaze at her and thought of holding her next to him … in his bed.

Jessie's eyes darted to the side. She blushed and sipped her tea. Her heightened color made him smile. He pushed off from the counter. "The kids should be done packing their toys."

"Okay. Let's get them loaded." Her steps were quick as she left the kitchen—and the subject of beds. "Then we can finish the living and dining rooms." She turned to address the children. "Start packing your summer clothes while we load these toys."

Shannon, in charge of the permanent marker, tugged on Jessie's hand and pointed. "Look at Layla's boxes."

Corbin stood behind Jessie and saw four boxes with princesses drawn on the sides. The light reflected off their dresses. "That's cute, but why are they shiny?"

"'Cause I added glitter glue!" Layla, always proud of her actions, jumped and clapped.

Jessie tossed her head back to stare at the ceiling. Corbin stood close enough her hair brushed his shoulder. She sighed and closed her eyes.

He pushed his fingers through her hair and rubbed the back of her neck. "It's fine. I'll set them outside and they'll either dry or freeze. Then we'll load them."

She seemed content to let him continue rubbing her neck, but they had work to do. As he stepped around her to grab a box, she sighed again. He glanced back. She moved her gaze from him to her daughter, but not before he caught the look of disappointment.

"Layla," Jessie held out her hands, "give me the glue. You're done using it for a while. You know the rule is to ask first."

"But I thought … okay." She handed over four bottles. All glittery and girly colored.

When they returned to the main room, Corbin shook out a newspaper and wrapped a ceramic bird.

"I guess I should ask first. Is this okay to put in a box?"

"Yeah. Everything in here is."

Corbin regretted picking up the delicate item, afraid his large hands would break it. "Pastor Wade reserved the date. I figured you'd want Tara to stand up with you. If so, then I'll ask Brock."

She nodded slowly. "When you set your mind to something, you mean to get it done."

"That's why I'm the foreman."

Her lips turned up as she continued filling boxes.

He hoped her smile stayed in place when he shared what else the pastor had to say this morning. But somehow he knew it wouldn't. "Um, you know how we thought the Sunday after Thanksgiving would be an ideal date to tie the knot?"

Jessie frowned.

Had he said something wrong? Lots of people referred to marriage that way. This already wasn't starting off well. He glanced at the ball of paper in his hands. How many sheets of newspaper had he used? Feeling foolish, and overwhelmed with nerves, he set it aside.

"What's wrong? Does the pastor want us to push back the date?" She raised her brows, probably in hopeful expectation.

"No, more like the opposite. Since Wade's spending Thanksgiving at the shelter like we are, his in-laws have planned a family holiday the Sunday after."

"On *our* day?"

He nodded. "And next weekend he's traveling to see his family. So … Pastor Wade suggested this Sunday."

She blinked in shock. "Tomorrow!"

***

Jessie methodically moved through the next room, trying to avoid Corbin as much as possible. He must have known she needed time to herself, because he left to check on the children's progress.

Her chest seized with anxiety. *Tomorrow!* How could they marry so soon? She wasn't ready to be his wife.

Why couldn't they make it a different day? Why did Pastor Wade even suggest tomorrow? Her temper flared. Good thing he wasn't here, or she'd tell him exactly what she thought.

Stomping to the calendar, Jessie ran her finger over the dates. She wished Shannon knew what days she'd be at play practice. Surely there was someone to call to find out. Thursday was already not an option. The shelter planned to officially open their doors from only serving lunch to providing overnight accommodations. She'd be there all day.

"Jessie," Corbin found her still at the calendar. "I've checked about other openings, either they don't work with our schedule or they don't work with Wade's."

He shoved a ball cap on his head. "The kids are hungry and so am I. I think I'll grab us some lunch."

"Fine." She brushed past him to a solid oak end table. She needed something to absorb her frustration. Shoving her arms beneath the overhanging top, she managed to lift it a few inches from the floor and waddle toward the door. Ugh. Jessie set it back down. Although she'd emptied its cabinet, it was still too heavy. Determined and stubborn, she walked it back and forth on its legs.

"And leave the heavy stuff to me." Corbin grabbed the cabinet from her hands and hefted it up as though it weighed no more than a toddler.

She watched him leave and mimicked, "*Jessie*, don't lift anything heavy. *Jessie*, don't drive anyone home by yourself. *Jessie*, you're going to marry me tomorrow." She stomped her foot. "Err, that man!"

She clomped upstairs to her office and plopped onto the worn out love seat positioned across from her desk. Richard had stuck the piece of furniture there as a way to avoid hauling it off. Mindlessly, she scratched at the hardened paint left on the arm by one of the kids. This couch wouldn't be going with them. The hide-a-bed sofa had outlived its purpose … but it would offer a homey atmosphere to the shelter and provide an extra bed.

Her fingernails stilled against the paint as an idea came to her. Without the mattress, the solid couch would lighten up considerably. Now was the perfect time to prove to Corbin she could manage perfectly well without his irritating list of instructions.

Where could she find a rope long enough to use as a pulley?

In the garage, she didn't find a rope, but she did find an orange extension cord. Jessie hurried back upstairs, almost giddy to prove how capable she was. She unfolded the bed and removed the mattress, making sure to put the slick side to the floor. Corbin would soon realize that with ingenuity such as hers, there was nothing she couldn't do. After she folded the hide-a-bed hardware back inside, she pushed the sofa away from the wall and rolled it onto the mattress. No lifting required. She tied a slip knot in the cord and slipped it around the couch then cinched it tight.

With a hand on her hip, she stood back and smiled at her well laid out plan.

The newel post would serve as part of her pulley system. The beam rose all the way to the white tongue and groove ceiling. She'd enjoyed living in this house, and could understand why the current buyers wanted it so badly. If they'd known Corbin's held more attention to detail, they probably would've sought after his.

The steady staccato of Corbin's diesel fueled truck announced his return. She went to the window and watched his strong legs extend from the cab. In her mind she could already see his powerful torso and bulging arms before he emerged.

She looked back and ran a tongue over her bottom lip. If she wanted to accomplish this on her own, she'd better hurry.

Since the post was rounded, she wouldn't have to worry about corners cutting into the cord's orange insulation. The cord slid easily between the post and spindle of the railing. She held fast then with a shove watched the loveseat slide down the first couple of stairs.

The weight pulled heavily against Jessie's hold, drawing her closer to the post. She stepped back to regain her position. Her foot stumbled on the couch cushion left on the floor, and prevented her other foot from finding a secure footing. She tripped. The couch slid faster. She righted herself but it was too late. Momentum had gained control.

Jessie yelped. Her plan was out of control. The force yanked her forward into the post.

With a throbbing lip, Jessie staggered back as the front door opened. She threw a hand to her temple as the couch flew off the mattress and slid to a stop at Corbin's feet.

His mouth drew in a tight line. "*What* are you doing?"

The image of her knight in armor crumbled with his scorn. But why had she expected anything different? Like a mischievous imp, she was doing exactly what he'd told her not to … knowing he'd be displeased. "I don't expect you to move everything. Not when I can easily do it myself."

Liar, liar. Your lip burns like fire.

***

While the children ate, Jessie studied her reflection in the bathroom mirror. She should've never tried to move the couch. Wasn't there a verse that said something about God giving the people over to their stubborn hearts to follow after their own counsel? It hadn't worked out too well for them, and it wasn't working out for her either. *Save me from myself, God.*

Corbin pushed through the partially open door. "How is—oh." He shook his head and whistled through his teeth. "I take it you were biting your lip when you hit the pole."

"How'd you—"

"You always do when you concentrate."

He knew this much about her? She lowered her gaze and fought a sudden urge to cry.

"Here," he held out a wet cloth drizzled with what appeared to be honey, "hold this against it."

She felt his constant stare but couldn't bring herself to look him in the eye. If he was waiting for an apology, she didn't owe him one. A grown woman, well past the age of needing instruction, Jessie wasn't about to regress because of one overbearing man.

"If you tell me what you want to do about the big furniture, I can take care of it while you shop for a dress."

Why did he have to be so thoughtful when she felt anything but? She glanced back at the mirror. "I'ine not goin any'ere like d'ish." She couldn't even form words, why would she want to shop for a pretty dress. A tear pooled in the corner of her eye. She brushed past him and wiped it away.

Layla left the table and circled her arms around Jessie in a big hug. "Mommy, you're 'till pretty."

A pitiful laugh tickled Jessie's throat. She'd been worried about correcting her daughter's speech and now she, too, couldn't pronounce her "s" blends.

"Tank you, 'oney."

The other children covered giggles they knew would create trouble. That was it. She wouldn't say another word until she could talk properly.

***

Hours later, the children climbed from the truck with their coats fastened and raced each other to the back of Corbin's house. Though it was cold, Jessie knew the fresh air would do them good and also free Corbin and her to unload without distraction.

Trails of dust left by a broom testified the garage had recently been swept. The wall showed a pattern of lighter squares in the paint where boxes had been stored. What had he moved to make room for her things?

Corbin brushed by with a box in each arm and lined them along the wall.

Jessie followed him inside the garage. "Thank you. For making room for our stuff."

"Of course."

He often answered like that. As if doing things for her was never a nuisance. A spark of hope sent an ember to her heart.

They stacked the boxes of toys along the back wall. Corbin passed her to retrieve another box while Jessie positioned hers. She pushed a plastic tub over to make room, yet still lacked an inch or two for her box.

On the other side of the tub, an engine dangled from a metal contraption. Jessie moved to its other side and pulled. It didn't budge. *Whew. This is heavy.* She tried again, this time shoving it from side to side.

Corbin returned with his arms full and came to a sudden stop. "No. Don't!"

Jessie followed his worried gaze to beneath the engine. Black ooze slopped over the side of a stained shop bucket she hadn't seen 'til now. She lurched forward but caught her foot on the bar of metal. As she fell, her hand knocked against the side of the pail tipping it the rest of the way.

Corbin's groan sickened her as much as the slippery oil staining the garage floor. Would she ever be able to do anything right?

Chapter Seven

Corbin dropped his boxes on top of the others along the wall and grabbed the half empty bag of kitty litter. Before the oil could spread too far, he shook out the contents.

"I didn't know you had a cat."

He sighed and shook his head. "I don't. The litter is for shop spills."

"Oh, so you've done this before, too?"

He couldn't keep the sarcasm from his voice. "Not quite. My spills are small in comparison to yours."

"Sorry for trying to help." She thrust an arm over toward the engine stand. "I just wanted to move that contraption so my box would fit."

"Then next time ask. You don't have to prove anything. I know what you're capable of and what you're not."

Her arms crossed over her chest as her weight shifted to one hip. "Excuse me?"

As usual, he'd done it again. He rubbed his temple to ease away a sudden pain. Jessie could be as prickly as a cactus. He jabbed his chest. "Me, boy." He pointed to her. "You, girl."

"So He-Man doesn't think *girl* is strong enough to do much, huh?" She paced a slow circle around him. "And you probably think my whole role in this farce of a marriage is going to revolve around the kitchen and the kids."

There wasn't any way he could answer her correctly, not the way she had him boxed in. But she wouldn't stop until he'd said something. "Jessie, first of all, this marriage isn't a farce. *Don't* call it that. Secondly, I. Don't. Want. You. Getting. Hurt. Is that plain enough?"

He spun from the garage before she could answer. Where did she get off referring to their marriage like that? She'd said yes on her own, he hadn't coerced her. She'd even admitted to praying about it.

There was no telling with women.

He grabbed another load in his arms and returned to the garage. Jessie passed him on her way to the truck. They continued working in silence until the bed was empty.

"Dad, we're hungry!" Garret stood at the open door to the house, letting in cold air.

"We're coming. I'll heat up the leftover chili." His son ran back inside as Corbin held the door and waited for Jessie to step through first.

"Thanks."

Her one word acknowledgement confused him. Either she was spouting off like a fire hydrant or kinked and dripping. One way or another, they had to find a balance.

Inside, he slipped off his boots and washed up at the sink. Jessie's neck craned in every direction as she walked through the kitchen. Had she been this far in his house before? Corbin couldn't remember.

He slipped the pan from the refrigerator to the stove then cleared his throat as he stirred the chili. "If you don't like the color, we can change it."

Jessie's mouth turned into the sly smile that always made him anticipate a smart retort. This was the part of their relationship he enjoyed most. Light hearted bantering.

"If I do choose to paint, I don't want your big feet in my pan."

He chuckled. "Aw, it'd be okay. I'm sure any mess we made would clean up with some oil."

Jessie's shoulders shot forward with her laugh. "*Oh*, my lip." Her hand briefly touched her mouth before she focused back on him. "You got me there. Guess we're even."

Nope. Not even close. But this time he was smart enough not to say it out loud. They were finally on good terms again and it was too close to the wedding to get her riled. He tested the warmth of the chili by bringing the spoon to his lips.

"Does your family always have to eat after you?"

"No. 'Cause after tomorrow, they'll also be eating after *you*." He crossed his arms and tapped his chin. "I seem to recall you saying something about looking forward to cooking and taking care of the kids."

Her face pinched in a cute, youthful expression as her eyes judged his humor. At last she waved him off. "Whatever."

He pulled out six bowls then Jessie spooned the chili. "Your lip looks a lot better."

Jessie's tongue darted across the cut. "Yeah, some. How'd you know to use honey?"

"Tara said it reduces swelling and has natural antibiotic stuff in it."

"Tara? When did you talk to her?" Chili slopped down the side of the bowl as Jessie waited for his response.

"I called when you were in the bathroom looking at your lip. I also figured you hadn't talked to her about tomorrow. Now it's taken care of."

***

Corbin said good night to his kids then stepped out the front door to breathe in the cool air. He'd dropped Jessie and her children off almost an hour ago, and it had taken that long for Shannon and Garret to settle down enough for bed. Did Jessie have the same problem?

He glanced down the street toward her house. All the lights were off except for one. Her bedroom. It could be she was still packing. Corbin hoped Jessie wasn't having troubling thoughts. Her comment about their marriage still bothered him. Why would she think it was a farce? What more did she want?

A cold blast of wind crept up his jacket sending a shiver through his frame. Time to go inside. He locked the door behind him and crept to the room that had been his office. Now his file drawers and desk were in the basement and this room would be Layla's. Although the boys were eager to share a room, Shannon was older. She was excited about the prospect of having Jessie as a mother, but he didn't think making her share a room with a six year old princess would benefit their situation.

77

He stared at the white walls. Jessie loved bold colors and did a good job painting. She and Layla would probably hatch a plan to change this room. But he wasn't sure he could tolerate Pepto-Bismol pink.

***

"Luke chapter fourteen says, *"But when thou makest a feast, call the poor, the maimed, the lame, the blind ..."*

Pastor Wade looked over the congregation. "I'm pleased to know that many of you are willingly doing this. A week from this Thursday, as we celebrate a season of thankfulness for all the Lord's blessings, several of you will be serving shoulder to shoulder with me and my family at the old community building."

Jessie fidgeted with the edge of her Bible, flipping the pages past her finger in a repetitive motion. Her nerves were knotted like a cheap ball of yarn. In less than two hours, she would become Mrs. Jessie Vaughn. Her stomach tightened. *Lord, I don't feel ready.*

Corbin's eyes darted toward her lap for the third time. He sighed and crossed his arms over his chest. If her restless behavior was distracting, why didn't he hold her hand? After all, he was the reason for her jitters.

"And in Isaiah," the pastor continued to say, "we read that we're also supposed to open our houses to them. Which is what we'll be doing at the shelter. This week we're opening the doors to provide overnight accommodations to those who need a boost to get back on their feet."

Pastor Wade closed his Bible and clutched it close as he paced behind the pulpit. "Have you ever wondered what it would be like to be homeless? What if you lost everything because of a bad money deal, or had your identity stolen? There are many variables we could touch on and whether you have the imagination to picture this or not, God paints a clear picture in His Word.

"Jesus's disciples were homeless. They were told to leave everything behind. Jesus wanted to grow their faith. And as Scripture clearly reveals, the disciples were slow to believe Jesus was more than a prophet. So to build their belief, he first took them away from what they were most dependent on, everything they owned.

"What do you depend on the most? If God has been dealing with you on a certain topic and you're avoiding Him, watch out. He can easily get your attention … the hard way. What might God need to take so you'll listen?"

"Mommy?"

Jessie turned to Layla who'd refused to go to her children's church class.

"I need to use the baf'room." She bounced on the cushioned pew.

She would have to choose now when I finally focused on the sermon. "Okay," Jessie whispered, "follow me."

In the bathroom, Jessie opened the handicapped stall to make room for both of them. Although her daughter was old enough to use it on her own, if not corrected, she still rested her hand on the bowl between the split. Jessie couldn't chance Layla rubbing her nose before washing her hands.

A little too cautious of germs, she pulled a string of toilet paper off to line the seat before Layla could sit. When she turned to give her daughter privacy, a dress bag hanging on the stall door caught her attention.

Huh. Tara must have brought a different dress to change into. She looked down at her full length black and white maxi skirt she'd worn with a white sweater. Tara shouldn't have gone to the trouble.

Temptation urged her to peek inside. Just as her hand raised, Layla announced she was done.

"Okay, let's get your hands washed."

When they returned to the sanctuary, the choir was singing the closing hymn. Corbin moved to the aisle to allow them to reenter the pew. His smile seemed pensive. Was he nervous, too, or just wondering about her thoughts? Whatever his worries, he deserved to have them. Why couldn't he have placed his hand over hers when she was fidgeting? What was wrong with the man that he never touched her?

Her thoughts escalated until she felt sick.

Pastor Wade thanked everyone for coming then made the announcements. "And you're welcome to attend Corbin Vaughn and Jessie Thompson's wedding in an hour. Refreshments following."

"Refreshments? I didn't make anything," Jessie mumbled to herself.

Corbin shrugged. "Maybe some of the ladies from church did."

She excused herself and hurried to the bathroom. Standing over the sink, the sick feeling faded, leaving her almost disappointed.

The door swung open and Tara entered. "Take deep breaths." She breathed deeply.

"Oh, quit. It's not like I'm having a baby."

"No. That type of breathing would be much faster." Tara dropped a loaded duffel bag on the floor and proceeded to clutter the sink basin with every form of female necessity.

"What's all this for? I'm just marrying my neighbor." Fear of Tara's intentions rose inside her.

"Uh, huh. Corbin is *not* just a neighbor. He's the kind of guy who would call your best friend and ask her what to do for his little pumpkin's lip." She pointed.

Jessie immediately ran her tongue over her ugly, bruised and split lip. "He did not call me his pumpkin."

"No. I added that for emphasis. But seriously, you'll soon realize he's a good man."

Tara turned them both toward the mirror. "He asked me to stand up with you at the ceremony."

Jessie tossed her head back in a helpless gesture. Why would anyone make a big deal out of this? This *ceremony* was just two widowed people making their lives work a little easier … or so they hoped.

"And …" Tara moved to the handicapped stall door and trailed a hand down its length. "Behind door number three is the dress that your *neighbor* asked me to purchase for his bride."

No way. He didn't.

Tara flung the door back, the dress bag swung from the movement.

"Go ahead. It's your holiday." Tara stood back and waited for Jessie's numb feet to move forward. When they didn't, she huffed in frustration and removed the garment.

Jessie sucked in air and covered her mouth. Before her very eyes was the ivory crocheted dress she'd admired for weeks. Her hands reached out, almost on their own volition, and traced the soft pattern of floral and scalloped tiers.

Jessie swallowed and looked up at Tara. They both batted droplets on their lashes. "How'd he know?"

"I don't know. I didn't tell him."

They had both admired the dress and spoke of it often, but never in the presence of Corbin.

"He just told me that was the one I should buy. And of course, Mr. Ever-So-Proper has already paid me back."

Jessie stared at the vintage styled dress. So that's the real reason he'd called Tara. She pressed her fingers past the crochet and touched the softness of the stretch lining.

"Well, we don't have all day. Try it on!" Tara pushed her into the stall.

The dress slid on easily and hugged her curves in a gentle manner. She stepped from the stall and gasped at her reflection. "Oh, I love it!"

"Me, too!" Tara smiled brightly and clasped her hands together. "It's so pretty I'd almost be willing to marry Justin again!"

Jessie laughed. "But you're still married to Justin."

"Uh, huh. But if given the choice, I doubt I'd do it again." Tara busied herself at the sink, setting out cosmetics and checking the heat of the curling iron.

Her comment returned the heaviness in Jessie's stomach. Although Tara tried to hide her unhappiness, anyone could see that she and Justin were having trouble.

Oh, God, don't let that be Corbin and me in a few years. Stop this wedding if things are only going to get worse.

Tara turned and slapped Jessie's restless hands. "Stop worrying. Corbin and Justin are nothing alike."

"What …"

"Forget it." Tara sloughed if off as though her problems were no big deal. "Today is your day."

"Boy, for best friends, we have some major communication problems."

Tara snorted and pushed a head band in Jessie's hand. "Put this on and clear that hair out of your face." She peered closer. "What'd you do to your makeup this morning, put it on in the dark?"

Jessie studied her reflection. It hadn't been dark, and her makeup wasn't that bad, but stress had definitely done a number to her skin's pallor.

Typical of a trained beautician and cosmetologist, Tara's skilled hands made a quick improvement. "Sorry, but I can't do much with your lip. The color would only cake in your cut and draw unwanted attention."

Too impressed with the changes in her looks to care about her lip, Jessie touched a gentle finger to her face. "How'd you make my color come back?"

"It's called bronzing powder. Honestly, Jessie, you should at least know that."

"Between the kids and my failing house payments, I haven't paid attention to much of anything." Maybe if she had, she would've seen the trouble in her friend's life. She watched Tara in the mirror.

"Whatever you're fretting about let it go. And if it's about me then don't worry yourself. Justin and I have always gone through ups and downs. We'll get through this one the same as all the others."

"How?"

"Didn't you listen to the message this morning?" Tara rolled a lock of Jessie's hair on the heated iron.

Part of it. The other part was spent with Layla. "All I know is I've been so absorbed in my own problem of agreeing to a loveless marriage that I never noticed my friend might be battling the same thing."

Tara removed the iron from Jessie's hair and stepped back. She rummaged through her purse then popped a piece of gum in her mouth. Experience had taught Jessie this was Tara's way of controlling what she said.

"We're not talking about me," she smacked. "Not today. Period."

"Great. Now you sound as bossy as Corbin."

"So what if he's not all lovey-dovey. I say if your man comes home to you every night, trusts you with his pay, and doesn't yell and holler, then he's worth keeping."

"I don't know if he's any of those things. Until now he's been the dad of kids I babysit."

"And pigs fly."

Jessie narrowed her eyes. It'd been a while since they had a spat, guess they were overdo. "Don't start running your mouth."

"I'm a people watcher. I work with people. I know how to read people. You obviously don't." Tara picked up another lock of Jessie's hair, losing her gentle touch, as her jaw worked the gum harder. "The man's held your attention for a while now. There's no shame in it. Especially now that you've agreed to marry him."

"Just chew your gum."

Tara curled the rest of Jessie's hair in silence. Jessie closed her eyes. *Show me where I'm wrong, God, even if I don't want to see it.*

The pastor's voice repeated in her mind. *"What might God need to take so you'll listen?"* Was that why He'd allowed the sale of her house? There was no doubt God approved of this marriage. It could be the house ordeal had been set in motion for this very thing … whether or not she wanted to see it.

Before she opened her eyes, she thought of Tara. Although Jessie didn't know what she was going through, she didn't have to know to be a friend. She swallowed hard. "Tara, I'm sorry I snapped at you. You've been here for me through so much."

"Yep. And after all I did today, do *not* start crying and ruin your makeup."

Their eyes met in the mirror. Jessie laughed and blinked back tears then dropped her jaw as she noticed her reflection. "Wow ... look what you've done." Hair draped over her shoulders in big, loose curls and shiny strands framed her face in a luminous glow. "I don't know how you did it."

"Trade secret. You could've watched and learned, but you slept through it all." Tara lightly teased. "Okay. I think I hear the start of pi'anny music."

Jessie left the comfort of the bathroom and followed Tara to the closed doors of the sanctuary. Why was there piano music? This was a second marriage for both of them. She expected they'd simply meet the pastor at the front of the church and exchange vows. Her thoughts were halted by Layla and Shannon, as they oohed and awed over her appearance.

The next few moments went by in a blur as the girls, followed by Tara, and then Jessie walked to the front of the church. Surprise stole her breath as she saw how many were in attendance. But nothing prepared her for the shock of her mother seated in the front row. Jessie stared in bemusement, as she walked past

Corbin reached for her arm to guide them to their places. The searing heat of his touch made butterflies dance in her stomach. No ... too dainty. She must've swallowed leaping frogs. *God, don't let me croak my vows!*

Corbin's eyes softened as he smiled down at her. He released her arm and clasped his hands together.

Jessie mindlessly toyed with the silk flowers Shannon had pressed in her hand. Where did they get the flowers anyway? Vera must have had something to do with it.

Corbin reached over and covered her hands with his. Jessie took a deep breath. Her nerves immediately calmed and the flowers stilled.

Then he let go.

Chapter Eight

After the wedding, Jessie followed Corbin's suggestion and changed into work clothes. They needed to move the kids' beds before evening. She grabbed a pair of jeans and her red and black button up shirt. Her hands stilled near the bottom of the row of buttons. The second to last button had fallen off and she hadn't replaced it. She couldn't fit in replacing a simple button in a year, yet Vera managed to throw together a wedding reception with less than a day's notice. She'd said the secret was in delegating. If that worked, Jessie had a whole basket of mending for someone.

She tied the ends of her shirt together then caught her reflection in the bedroom mirror. Wedding hair didn't exactly go with flannel. She grabbed her hair in one hand and looked for an elastic band. Nothing.

Corbin was already inside when she entered the living room. "You should leave it down."

"What?" Jessie looked behind her then realized he referred to the hair she held. "I guess I'll have to. I can't find a ponytail holder."

He smiled as her hair fell around her shoulders. A tiny flutter stirred low in her belly. The moment ended all too soon as Corbin clapped his hands together. "Let's get this done."

She glanced at the ceiling as he turned to the kids' rooms. *You said to marry him, God. And I did. But I think we're going to need some help.*

Once the beds were disassembled, moved, and reassembled, Jessie was ready to quit. Her feet ached, her arms were tired, and her mood plummeted.

Corbin joined her in the hallway as Shannon helped Layla arrange her things and the boys dumped their collection of Legos. "Now all that's left is to move your clothes into our room."

Jessie turned with him and stood in the entrance of the master bedroom. The amphibians returned, playing leapfrog in her middle. She stared at his bed. "You don't expect us to share that, do you?"

Corbin rested his forearm against the other side of the door frame. His mouth rose in a curious smile as he looked from the bed to her. "Uh, yeah. That's what husbands and wives usually do."

"But you haven't even held my hand!" Her voice came across stronger than normal.

Corbin turned and leaned his back against the frame, narrowing the space between them. "You want me to ... hold your hand?"

Fully indignant, Jessie squared her jaw and faced him. "If you expect to hold anything else, that would be a good place to start."

***

As if in a race, Jessie readied herself for bed in record time. Dressed in her usual attire of plaid pajama bottoms and an old T-shirt, she climbed under the covers before Corbin could enter. In a sitting position, she pulled her hair to the side and separated it into three strands as Corbin took his turn in the master bathroom.

The lamp on his side cast a warm glow around the room. Enough to take in his strong physique as he stepped into the room.

"That's all you're wearing?" Jessie stared at his boxer shorts clad body.

"Yep."

His one word answer grated on her nerves. Although she would've preferred to keep staring, she pulled her eyes away from his thick-muscled form and rolled to her side.

A soft thud sounded against the wall, followed by another. She looked over her shoulder. Corbin tossed off the pillows she'd carefully lined to separate her half of the bed from his. "What are you doing?"

"Removing the Great Wall of China," he huffed. The mattress dipped as he climbed in. "This is no way to start out a marriage, Jessie."

She kept her back turned and remained quiet. His lips had barely touched hers at the wedding and now he expected her to swoon toward him? What planet was he from anyway?

***

Jessie yawned and leaned backward with her hands on her hips. Muscles she hadn't used in years cried out in complaint. The new owners wanted to move in by the end of the week, if possible. She didn't see how it could work out, but would try. She probably should have started at this house, but instead had cleaned Corbin's most of the morning.

The doorbell rang. Jessie glanced at her dusting mittens. The dollar-find worked beautifully for dusting floor moldings and door tops. She tossed them against the wall and answered the door.

"Hi, Crystal." Familiar with one another from church, Jessie invited the curly blonde inside.

"Wow, it's so empty. Such a difference from when you and Robert held the Christmas parties ... oh, how thoughtless. I'm sorry to bring that up, Jessie."

"It's okay." They stood in awkward silence, neither knowing what to say. Jessie finally pointed toward her room. "You want to see the bedroom suite and make sure it's what you want?"

"Sure."

They stepped inside and Crystal trailed a hand over the plain Quaker style bed. Every piece, from the long dresser with the square mirror hanging above on the wall to the bedside tables matched the simplistic design that Richard had appreciated. She couldn't understand why he thought the set would look nice in their home but hadn't wanted to disappoint him by her objection. Instead, she'd satisfied herself with purple walls.

"I can't believe the new owners didn't want this." Crystal's voice held a true sense of awe. "I'm so glad. This is exactly what I've been looking for."

Jessie smiled. "Great. When can you move it?"

"Dean said we could come back tonight if that's okay with you."

Jessie agreed and they walked back toward the door. She was glad someone wanted the furniture. They were too well made not to be appreciated, but she'd never liked their appearance. Corbin's, on the other hand, were more her taste. The high, dark cherry headboard contrasted well with the light tan walls of his bedroom. Which surprised her, as she'd never considered the color on any of her walls.

The decision to keep his furniture and sell hers was easily agreed upon. It was funny how they could agree on some things while others caused outlandish disputes.

"I guess Alyssa couldn't make the wedding?"

Crystal's comment grabbed Jessie's attention. "I didn't notice."

By the way Crystal watched her reaction, was she aware of the crush the other woman seemed to have on Corbin?

Tempted to ask, Jessie's opportunity ended as Crystal opened the door. "Thanks so much for the fair price. It's really nice of you. And I wish you and Corbin the best."

Left alone, Jessie tried to slough off the melancholy feeling Crystal's question had left, but the thought continued to nag her as she cleaned. Was she wrong not to consummate the marriage last night, especially if she already had competition? Yet how could she have? Their whole relationship was awkward at best. Of course, they had moments of building intimacy. If a few seconds qualified as a moment. But as if out of fear, Corbin was quick to extinguish them. What could he be afraid of?

Jessie's stomach growled and reminded her she hadn't eaten breakfast. Now it was almost noon and there was nothing to eat in the house. She grabbed her coat and walked toward Corbin's—and her—house. The idea still didn't feel natural. Everything had moved so fast.

Inside the kitchen, she learned what he meant when he said his refrigerator wouldn't be as clean as hers after only owning the appliance for three months. The glass shelves were dirty with dried milk, food smudges and what looked like scattered spices or dried up lettuce. She couldn't tell. No longer hungry, she took everything out and, starting at the bottom, removed the drawers, then the shelves and so forth. By the time she had the appliance cleaned and reloaded, all she wanted was a nap.

Jessie stretched out on her stomach across the carpeted living room and sighed. Too tired to think about her current situation, she only wanted to rest. Starting with her arms, she mentally relaxed the muscles and worked her way down to her legs until she was at a complete state of relaxation.

***

The extended parking lot would never be finished if he didn't focus. Corbin prized his company on always meeting deadlines. That's what set them apart. And now because of an extended parking lot and … how did he describe his personal life? Married, yet not exactly husband and wife, he and Jessie's current arrangement kept him fully distracted.

He hurried through traffic and back home, opened the garage door and found the transit he'd forgotten this morning on the side of the garage kept for his things. He glanced over the packed adjacent wall. Something was different. The boxes were neater and more organized. Jessie must have cleaned, though he couldn't imagine when she'd had the time. He walked around the truck. Even the excess kitty litter had been swept up. Only a small portion remained.

In case she was inside, he didn't want her scared wondering who had entered the garage. He pulled out his keys to the door leading to the kitchen. It wasn't locked. He mentally sighed. The woman tempted fate at every turn, but then again, as long as the garage door was down this door shouldn't matter.

Inside, the kitchen gleamed. Nothing was left on the counter. The table was clear of clutter and even boasted a fall centerpiece. The cleanliness almost shamed him. Almost. He was a man, and not even his mother expected him to keep house the way she did.

"Jessie?"

No answer. Maybe she was at the other house.

He turned toward the living room and his heart fell to his feet. Strewn across the floor as though she'd passed out, Jessie laid on her side with her head lolled back from her shoulder and her mouth open. He dropped to his knees beside her unmoving form and rolled her over. Cradling her head, he croaked out her name, "Jes—"

Her lips smacked together with a contented sigh. As her arms slowly straightened outward, her hand barely missed slapping his face. Her legs stretched with her yawn then curled over his thighs.

She was sleeping?

Her eyes blinked opened. Jessie stared at Corbin with a blank expression before darting her focus around the room. "What are you doing? What's wrong?"

Worry rushed from his chest, and he didn't know whether to hug her to him or drop her head to the floor. "You were sleeping."

"No I wasn't." Jessie sat up and accepted Corbin's hands to pull her to her feet. She stretched again, arching her back.

Did she have any idea what she was putting him through? Emotionally ... and physically? He cleared his throat and forced himself to look away. "Why didn't you go back to bed if you were so tired?"

"I told you," she frowned, "I wasn't sleeping. I don't take naps during the day."

"Then what would you call that?" He followed her into the kitchen as she opened the refrigerator.

"Grabbing a few ... moments."

"Well your moments scared the tar out of me."

Laughter bubbled from her chest.

"What's so funny?" Though he didn't know, her lighthearted mood brought a smile to his face as well.

"You and ... tar! You're going to have to clean that up yourself!" She laughed again as she rummaged through the meat drawer.

He shook his head and glanced from what she was doing to the stove. Surprised again, she'd also cleaned his appliances. "Jessie, don't overwork yourself."

"Are you hungry?"

She dropped lunch meat on the counter then turned to retrieve something else. He stopped her with a hand over her arm and instantly regretted the action. Being near her was one thing, touching was quite another. Her skin warmed and pulsed beneath his hand. The stubborn woman was just as attracted to him as he was to her. "Stop working so hard. I don't want you making yourself sick."

Breaking contact, she crossed her arms over her chest. "For being such a tough guy, you sure have some fear issues."

He ignored her insinuation. "Who said I was a tough guy?"

"You know, 'cause of your strong construction build." She curled an arm and squeezed her bicep. Corbin wished she would've grabbed his.

Encouraged by her playfulness, he removed his insulated shirt. "You mean … *this* build?"

Her eyes darkened and never left his hands as he dropped the shirt to the floor and pulled on his undershirt. No kids were in the house. Maybe now she'd reconsider her decision of last night.

"Would you stop doing that?" Jessie huffed and looked away.

Corbin paused and let his shirt fall back in place. "Doing what?"

"Teasing me with your body." A blush crept up her neck.

He moved closer. "You could always even the playing field.'"

She turned to face him so quickly he stepped back. "You just don't get it."

In an instant, the room changed from warm to cold. Jessie grew quiet, climbing inside her shell.

What did she expect from him? He didn't think she was the type who wanted a smothering relationship.

Corbin pulled a deep breath and slowly released it. "I'll see you tonight."

Chapter Nine

"Hi, *Mom.*" Shannon was the last to step through the door. She leaned forward to embrace Jessie in a hug. "I like saying that."

"You're sweet. And I like to hear it." She rubbed her arms from the cold air and closed the door. "Did you have a good day?"

"Yep. And I found out when practice starts." She raised her brows. "Tonight."

"What? Why didn't they give us more notice?"

"Mrs. Walker had wanted to start tomorrow after school but something came up. And our next practice is on Wednesday."

"We go to church on Wednesdays."

"She said it would be over in time."

If Mrs. Walker knew folks would be concerned with practice interfering with church, why not schedule a different night? "Let's hope. Otherwise you'll have to leave early."

"After today, we'll stay late after school. Tonight is the only night it's late. But I like that about you, Jessie … I mean, Mom." Shannon dropped her chin a notch as she smiled. "You don't let others bully you. You stand up for what you believe."

"Thank you, hon'." She studied her closer. "Is somebody bothering you?"

Shannon started for her room. "Not really. They just don't get it."

"Don't get what?" Jessie asked her retreating form.

"Jesus." The answer came softly, almost indiscernible.

Was Shannon being bullied for her faith? Jessie's spine stiffened and her hands clenched at her sides.

"Mom, can me and Garret play outside?"

She glanced at her son's smiling face. "Sure. Just zip your jackets."

He ran past to the sliding, dining room door. Garret stopped long enough to give Jessie a brief hug. "Love you."

"Love you, too," she managed before her throat tightened. Guilt descended on her heart. The children eagerly accepted the change in their lives, while she still fought against it … or at least their father. She longed for a quiet place to pray.

"Mommy, I'm hungry." Layla stood in the kitchen. Still unfamiliar with Corbin's house, her eyes followed each cabinet door, not knowing what was inside.

"Let's see what we have for an afterschool snack." Jessie opened a cupboard and shoved aside cans of beans, vegetables, and boxes of noodles. Corbin could organize the tools in the garage but not a simple shelf of food.

Fatigue settled over Jessie's shoulders like a ton of bricks. Troubled by her marriage, Shannon's admission, and physically drained, all she wanted was to crawl into bed. But she couldn't. Not only did they have play practice, she still hadn't prepared anything for supper.

She pulled out a box of crackers. "Have some graham crackers and milk, while I come up with something for us tonight."

"Yay! Them's my favorite."

"*They're* my favorite."

"Right." Layla nodded as though approving Jessie's speech.

Jessie inwardly sighed. *One day, Lord. She'll catch on, one day.*

***

After a quick dinner of soup and grilled cheese sandwiches, Jessie left a note for Corbin, who was late because of a meeting, and hurried the kids back to school. This was one thing she hadn't prepared for, driving to functions for this many children. She and Corbin had to discuss how many extracurricular activities they allowed to interfere with family time. If they didn't, their lives would be ruled by the school system.

A few yards from their driveway, three cats bounded across the road. Jessie stomped the brakes. Her jaw clenched. Mrs. Clarkson faithfully fed every stray cat within a three mile radius. Unfortunately for those in the neighborhood, she did so by dumping her garbage in the gutter of the road. She'd been annoying simply as a neighbor, Jessie couldn't imagine the joy she'd have experiencing her as a *next* door neighbor.

She mentally checked off the items still on her list to do. "Oh no!"

"What is it?" Shannon looked at her with wide eyes.

"I forgot Crystal was coming for the bedroom furniture tonight."

Had her life ever been this busy before?

During practice, Jessie kept watch between Shannon and the three younger kids playing off to the side of the gymnasium. Who was mistreating Shannon? Whoever it was, they probably weren't involved in the Christmas play.

Mrs. Walker explained the program order and handed out the script then pulled the choir to the side and instructed what songs they were to sing. Jessie couldn't wait to hear Shannon's voice. She still remembered the few times she sang solos at church. The girl was blessed with a wide vocal range.

Her thoughts drifted back several hours, to waking up in Corbin's arms. He was right, she'd been asleep. A very good sleep, too. She dreamed they were walking hand in hand, looking at Christmas gifts for the kids. Her stomach did funny flips in response to his nearness coupled with his cologne of suede and cedar wood. Corbin said her name, then slid his hand beneath her hair behind her neck, drawing her to him. Though they were in a public shopping mall, he didn't hesitate as his lips drew nearer. Finally, they were going to kiss.

Then she'd awakened, nearly curled up in his lap.

Her skin warmed thinking of his insinuation in the kitchen. He possessed a playful side she hadn't been aware of and would love to enjoy. Yet she couldn't. Not if she wanted more than just a physical relationship. But that task wouldn't come easily.

Corbin didn't want to be close. Not emotionally. Perhaps the death of his wife had built the walls of protection around his heart. Having never met her, Jessie couldn't judge if he'd been different before or not.

Mrs. Walker thanked everyone for coming and announced it was time to leave. Jessie climbed down the bleachers and overhead Shannon's conversation with another student.

"The song's about the angels' singing over Jesus' birth," Jessie explained.

"My mom says Jesus isn't real. He's just another story like Santa Claus." The girl narrowed her eyes, as if challenging Shannon to refute her mother's logic.

"Like I told you, He's real to me." Shannon looked up and saw Jessie. "I have to go." She tugged on Jessie's hand and pulled them toward her siblings standing by the door.

God, I have to share this with Corbin. Help us pull together enough to guide Shannon. Speak through us and give her courage.

In the car, Shannon sat in the passenger front seat, quiet and pensive.

"Was that girl the one who troubled you earlier?"

Shannon turned toward the window. "Yes. We were listing our favorite Christmas songs." She drew lines in the condensation of the window. "She's talking about me to other kids. They call me a Jesus freak."

A spark of anger colored Jessie's vision. "Have you talked to the teacher?"

"What good would that do? I've talked to God, though."

"And what did He say?"

"I don't know. He hasn't gotten back with me yet." Her instant smile brightened the van's interior.

Jessie turned onto their street. Corbin, with Crystal's husband, Dean, carried the long bedroom dresser to a trailer behind Dean's truck. The bed and side tables were already loaded. She pulled beside the curb. "Stay in the van, kids, so you won't be in the way. I'll just be a minute."

Crystal waved as she caught up with her at the door. "All that's left is the mirror."

"I'm so glad Corbin was home to help."

"Me, too, and thanks for messaging me to let me know you wouldn't be here. I understand about being busy. Dean's mom is helping us out with the kids tonight." Crystal stepped back as the men reentered the house. "I gave the check to Corbin. Hope that's all right."

"Sure." Jessie's gaze followed her husband as he brushed by. Was he intent on his job, or did he ignore her on purpose?

"He seems pretty tired."

"He has a tight deadline to meet. When I called to ask him to meet you, he said the building committee wouldn't pay the overtime needed to finish the parking lot by Christmas, which sets him back on his next job."

"The world sure has gotten in a hurry hasn't it?"

Jessie heard Crystal, but Corbin's return caught her attention.

"Wow, you've got it bad." Crystal covered her laugh with her hand.

"What?" Jessie wanted to deny the statement. Corbin's gaze locked with hers. His gray-blue gaze consumed her. A tingle raced up Jessie's spine. Would tonight be different? All it would take for her to give in was a little show of emotion. Didn't he feel anything for her?

The evening rushed by in a frenzy of motion. The children hadn't seen Corbin all day and vied for his attention. Amidst the constant chatter of their voices, Jessie curled in a corner of the couch and felt the last of her energy fade. She snuggled deeper into the crook of the cushioned back and closed her eyes to the sound of play and giggles. The children's happiness comforted her soul into a dreamy state of peace.

When Jessie awoke, it wasn't to the sounds of children. Corbin was as noisy as a rooster in the henhouse out in the kitchen. She stretched and looked at the clock. She'd slept straight through the night. When had she gone to bed? Despite the early hour, she felt fully rested.

Jessie pushed back the covers. She still wore the clothes from yesterday. She must have really been tired if she couldn't remember going to bed *and* didn't change into pajamas. She grabbed clean clothes on the way to shower.

The warm water soothed as it needled Jessie's overworked muscles. Today she wouldn't push so hard … if she could keep from it. After washing her hair, she turned the water off. She leaned her head closer to the glass door. Why could she still hear running water?

Jessie peeked her head out of the sliding door, snagging a towel. "Corbin! What are you doing in here?"

"Shaving." Like before, his one word answer grated against her. He tapped his razor against the sink and brought it back beneath his chin.

"Why couldn't you wait? It's my turn." Inside the shower, she swiped the towel over her legs and wrapped it around her body.

"I have to be at work. You know that."

She slid the door back and brought a leg over the tub. "I thought you'd already been in here. I heard you in the kitchen."

"I started my coffee. Now it's my turn for the shower." His gaze met hers through the mirror. Though he still held the razor near his face, his eyes never wavered. "As long as you were taking, I thought we'd have to share the stall."

"Oh, you never quit." She rolled her eyes and hiked her other leg over the tub. Her toe stubbed the metal runner. Jessie tripped forward, hitting her elbow on the towel rack. Pain thrummed all the way to her shoulder and momentarily paralyzed her arm, making it impossible to control her fingers. "Ooh, I hit my funny bone."

Corbin didn't answer. Nor did he acknowledge her pain. Jessie glanced over at him. His gaze magnetized on her body. A silly smile pulled at his mouth. He seemed to be … drooling. In horror Jessie realized she'd dropped her towel.

"Close your eyes!" She grabbed her only covering off the floor and wrapped the towel around her, clinging to the ends as if they were a lifeline.

Though Corbin's eyes were tightly closed in obedience, he smiled warmly. "I can still see you."

"Oh, stop it." Mortified, Jessie wanted to blend into the wall. No chance of that happening now. She scooped up her clothes.

"Why worry with those?" He put down the razor and moved toward her, bringing with him the clean scent of shaving cream.

Jessie's hand pressed against his T-shirt clad chest. "Remember saying, you, man," then she pointed to herself, "me, woman? Well this woman doesn't have a one-track mind."

"We're married." Corbin heaved one shoulder. "I don't see the problem."

Her fingers dug into the towel for strength. "You need to show me some affection before any of this." She motioned between them.

Corbin's dulled gaze didn't help her argument.

"Is that so difficult?" When she didn't get a response, she added, "What do you have to lose?"

Familiar grief saddened his gaze. Was he withholding his feelings to protect himself should something happen to her like it had his first wife? She gasped, "You're thinking, what if I die?"

Something akin to anger rose inside her. "And what then? Pain? Is it any better to *live* pain?

Because this doesn't fit my idea of living or a marriage."

Corbin turned and started the shower, as if he had no intention of answering her.

Jessie continued. One way or the other, this man had to talk. She needed an explanation. "You've never held my hand. Except at the wedding, you've never kissed me. In fact, you hardly ever touch me."

He finally faced her and huffed, "I don't want that type of relationship."

Had she heard him right? "You mean ... love?"

"Well, yeah." He scratched his chest above his heart. "You know what it's like. It only leads to hurt."

She found it hard to swallow. His confession was like a blow to the chest. Jessie forced out the question. Did she really want the answer? "So is that why you asked me to marry you and not Alyssa? I'm easier not to love?"

"Who—what? No! It's not that at all. I just think it's better to have a marriage based on friendship."

She didn't know anyone who thought like this. What kind of marriage did he have before?

Every emotion she possessed collided together in her heart and mind. "That works if you like living as a *monk*." She brushed past him to the dimly lit bedroom. With her back toward the bathroom, she angrily hoped he was watching. The towel fell to the floor and she quickly dressed. She looked back on her way out the door to see his slack jaw. "Let me know how that works out for you."

***

"Thanks for calling me back, Tara." Jessie stopped outside her mother's workplace and paced the concrete while she talked on her cell phone. "You won't believe what happened this morning."

She divulged the morning's events, hoping for support and justification.

"Sounds like a good script for a soap opera." Her mother's raspy voice startled Jessie. She spun around to see the office window opened. "Mom!"

"Hurry up and get in here, will you? It's cold eavesdropping in this weather."

Jessie rolled her head to the side with her eyes toward the sky. *Why me, Lord?* She pressed the phone back against her ear and addressed Tara, "I'll have to call you back."

Inside the retirement community's recreation room, Jessie's mother came forward and wrapped an arm around her shoulders. "Come to my office where there's less chance of busybodies adding their two cents worth."

"Oh, and you wouldn't know anything about that, huh?"

"Honey, I only listen in, rarely do I advise."

Jessie settled in a chair across from her mother's desk.

"Why'd you do it, baby? Why'd you marry him?" She tapped a cigarette on her desk, packing the tobacco near the end before striking her lighter.

"Won't they write you up if they find out you're smoking in here?" Although she knew it was hopeless to expect her mother to change habits, Jessie didn't want her losing her job.

Her mother smiled and blew smoke through the cracked window then pointed to a bowl in the corner behind her. "Remember how I used to fill a bowl with vinegar when we fried fish?"

"Yes. Does it absorb the smell of smoke, too?"

"How do you think I've kept my job?" She laughed and waved her hand as if to push the smoke out the window. "Now answer my question."

"Remember telling me why you married Max?" Jessie loved and respected her mother too much to share her mother's title of parenthood with someone who hadn't put forth the effort. Thus, her father was always Max.

Jessie waited for her mother's familiar nod. They quoted together, "It seemed like the thing to do at the time."

Her mother inhaled deeply from her cigarette and looked expectantly across the desk. She still waited for an answer.

Jessie shrugged. "I didn't have much of a choice, did I? You know the state I was in."

Thoughts from the evening before pushed aside the challenge of house payments and brought a smile to her lips. "I know by what you overheard you probably don't think the best of him, but he's a great dad. Last night, Layla asked him to play donkey and—"

"Donkey? Not horsy?" A loud laugh followed. "Oh, that's rich."

Jessie tried not to encourage her comment. "But though he'd worked late, he still got on his hands and knees and gave her a ride on his back." She laughed at the memory.

"I bet Layla enjoyed that." Her mother tapped the end of her cigarette in an ashtray hidden in a desk drawer.

"Uh huh. Corbin may not have once the boys joined in. They were pretty rough, but he never got upset." She chewed her bottom lip. He could show them affection, but not her.

The sudden desire to cry approached her like a rainstorm.

"I just wish he loved me back."

Chapter Ten

Two days had passed after Jessie's towel incident. Since then she didn't go near the shower until after Corbin left. Not that it mattered. He no longer toyed with her. He treated her like a sister. A distant sister.

Which wasn't at all what she wanted.

She stood in front of the open freezer and stared at the contents. They hadn't done any shopping since moving. Nothing to fix. At least nothing that seemed appealing. With a slight shove, she allowed the door to swing shut as she stepped back. Tonight was still a long way off, she'd figure something out by then.

Her purse lay on the floor beside the table where she'd dropped it after play practice last night. Jessie rummaged for the van keys as her thoughts ran over the conversation with Corbin last night. Lying in bed, she'd rolled over to talk. He was already facing her. Did he always lay toward her? Since she slept with her back to him, she had no way of knowing.

"Can't sleep?" he'd asked.

"No. I was thinking of Shannon."

"Why?"

"Some kids at school are giving her trouble over her faith." She picked at the corner of her pillow case, her hand within inches of his. "They call her a Jesus freak."

Even in the dark, she felt the change in Corbin. The air thinned as she waited for his response. Was he upset she'd forgotten to mention this until now? When he finally spoke, his words were clipped. "How long has this gone on?"

"I'm not sure. She told me about it Monday."

He rolled onto his back. "I'll talk to her."

For the first time since sharing his bed, Jessie had remained facing him. She'd waited to hear his breathing fall into the steady pattern of sleep, but it never did.

Her fingers brushed against the ridges of her keys. With them now in hand, she grabbed a card from a box of daily verses as she walked out the door. The cold interior of the van made her hands tremble as she read from Psalms. *"...commune with your own heart upon your bed, and be still."* Could this be what Corbin was doing as she waited for him to fall asleep?

Although she was no longer in bed, Jessie leaned back in the seat while the engine idled and warmed the interior. The verse spoke volumes. "God. I'm ready to talk about what's in my heart."

She swatted the card back and forth against her hand, stalling for time. But for what reason? God already knew her heart.

"I don't want this type of marriage. And ... *may*-be I was wrong to withhold from Corbin."

"Defraud ye not one another except it be with consent for a time…"

"Okay. So I admit it. That was wrong. I realize now if I'd trusted in You from the beginning, we'd probably be at the next level." Intimacy grew a marriage, and she had definitely stifled it by withholding. Corbin still wasn't providing what she wanted … his heart, but she also hadn't been very patient.

What was it her mother had said? Portions of yesterday's conversation replayed in her mind.

"Does he respect you?" Her mother had leaned forward with her elbows on the desk.

Jessie looked up, surprised by the question. "Of course. At least, I can't think of a time he hasn't."

"Well, I heard a guy on the radio once say that a man interprets respect as love. If that's true, then it makes sense he'd show it in the same way. Maybe he does love you, honey, but just doesn't know it yet. Some men are thick that way."

Jessie smiled to herself. Ignoring the way he corrected her foul ups, Corbin always treated her with respect. Maybe even more in the last year. Not to mention, he was always concerned for her health. Maybe the man liked her more than he wanted to admit.

If so, then they were quite the pair.

Despite not knowing what was ahead, her troubles lifted. Jessie left for the shelter and arrived eager for the day. She'd called Heather's motel to offer first dibs on the available family room, but the manager refused to give out information or pass on the message. With God's blessing, they'd be here today and Jessie could share the good news.

"Good morning, pretty bride." Vera opened the door and hugged Jessie as she stepped inside. "Brrr. I bet we get snow soon."

"Missouri weather keeps you guessing. You never know."

"Well said." Vera waved her hand. "Come see the furniture we added."

Past the cafeteria, in the sitting room, the plain wooden floor now featured a large rug beside a long, brown couch. "This is great. And I see someone donated a television."

"We're still short some furniture throughout, but I'm confident God will supply what we need."

Vera left Jessie as the voices of the other volunteers broadcast from the kitchen.

Jessie marveled at the change made by the additional walls, paint, and furnishings. She prayed as she passed each room for those who would benefit from the shelter. "Lord, fill this house with Your Holy Spirit. Let no evil enter in. May each soul find peace and sanctity while staying here and please guide each of us as we reach out to them. Amen."

Soon, the cafeteria was filled with the noise of hungry people. Jessie glanced about the room. Heather still hadn't arrived, but a familiar voice did reach out to her.

"Jessie."

"How are you today, Nevin?"

"Blessed."

Though he said the words, Jessie saw pain in his usually bright eyes. She took the seat next to him and covered his liver-spotted hand with hers. "But what's trying to steal those blessings?"

Nevin ran his teeth across his bottom lip and squeezed her fingers as he stared at the different faces in the room. "What makes you different, girlie? How can you smile like you do when you're surrounded with the rejects of society?"

A pang of sadness stabbed her chest. Who had upset this beautiful man? Nevin wasn't like most people she'd met through the shelter. He held onto an uncanny outlook of hope and eagerly shared his optimism with those he met. But someone, somewhere, had broken through his defenses.

She touched his scruffy face and turned his chin to meet her steady gaze. "I don't see any rejects. I come here to talk with friends and make new ones." She paused to smile at a teenage girl who sat down at the far end of their table. "I see humanity's beauty that's often hidden in a world spinning by too fast.

"And … I see hope." Her gaze returned and rested on Nevin. "Hope that encourages those who have none.

"Small-minded people will try to take that from you, Nevin, but don't give it up. It's *your* gift."

He leaned his head against hers for a brief moment and sighed.

Jessie whispered a prayer for their ears alone. "God, take away the hurt that Nevin is feeling. If it's from thoughtless words, remove them from his mind. Restore his hope in each day and strengthen him even more than before. So many people look to this man for encouragement, support, and love … including me. Thank you for bringing him here and crossing our paths. Amen."

Tears dripped onto the table where Nevin bowed his head. "I needed that, girl," he sniffed.

Concern and curiosity troubled her. The homeless were often mistreated by those who didn't understand. Because they lacked running water, soap, and simple bare necessities, people often used discriminating names and sometimes threw rocks or trash at them. But although Nevin wasn't rich by society standards, he wasn't homeless anymore. He had a roof over his head. What had happened?

"You go on now." Nevin wiped his eyes with the back of his sleeve. "You've been good to me, and now others need you. Go share that big smile and make someone else's day."

Love for her friend overwhelmed her. God was good in allowing her to be a part of his life. She would focus on that and continue to pray for him.

Jessie moved to greet a mother and her crying baby. "Hi, I'm Jessie." She wanted to hug the woman to let her know she was welcomed and accepted here, but the distrust in her eyes held Jessie back.

"Uh huh. And I'm just here to eat." She motioned to the door behind her. "Sign said you'all givin' out free food."

Jessie nodded. "We certainly are. Can I walk with you and hold your baby while you fill a tray?"

A short laugh slipped past her dry lips. "Ain't nobody ever asked to hold her. She's always crying.

So if you wanna, be my guest." She thrust the child into Jessie's arms.

In line, Jessie asked Marilyn for a warm cloth to wipe the child's face. While she hustled around in the kitchen to do as asked, Jessie watched the woman beside her. Vera had scooped a full ladle of soup into her bowl, yet the woman still held it out.

"Fill it up all the way. This got to last me a while." Her sleeves pulled back as her arms stretched forward. Scars riddled every visible part of her skin.

Jessie swallowed hard. She'd read about people who cut themselves on purpose. Slashing when emotional pain gets unbearable, they turn to physical pain as a means of control.

Jessie's problems shrunk in comparison to this woman's.

Marilyn returned with the warm cloth and a bottle but didn't hand it across the window where they served food. Instead, she came through the kitchen door and reached for the baby. Jessie looked back to see how the mother would react. She sat devouring the meal as though she'd not eaten in days.

***

Corbin tossed the grounds from his coffee cup onto a mound of dirt. Still bothered by the stubborn committee he'd met with last night, and the condition of his marriage, he couldn't wrap his head around anything at work.

As his crew clomped toward the trailer for lunch and a break from the cold, he stared across the parking lot toward the unfinished extension. Several small trees would have to be uprooted, the dirt worked back, and leveled before paving. Two days. Two days he'd start behind on his next job.

Corbin rubbed his temples and an idea came to him. Jessie mentioned a man, whose family lived in a motel room, worked construction in the city. He'd save money and time if he had a job in town. Corbin's idea built as Brock walked up and punched his arm.

"What are you moping about? And don't tell me it's the extended parking lot. You've met tighter deadlines before."

Corbin watched the remaining drop of brown liquid trail back to the bottom of his cup. "It's that and everything else."

"Jessie?"

As his closet friend, Brock would see through false bravado. Corbin might as well explain. Maybe the talk would do some good.

"You know what I've been through with the kids' mom. I don't want to go through that again." He rubbed a hand over his face, unconcerned for the dirt streaks he undoubtedly left. "She wants … well, you know … all that sentimental stuff."

"Huh?"

Corbin shrugged and waved his hand to the side. "Like holding hands and who knows what else."

The look on his friend's face said he still didn't understand. "So, what's the big deal?"

"The big deal is I don't want that." His hands chopped through the air, "But she won't consummate our marriage without it."

"What?" Brock's head tossed back with his loud, boisterous laugh. "Oh, I love this girl." He chuckled again. "Good, so your woman has spunk."

"Not good. We've both loved and lost so it makes sense to just keep things simple."

"Sounds to me like they are." He laughed more at Corbin's expense. "Man, you don't have a clue." Brock leaned forward. "To get what you want, you have to woo the woman. Forget the body for a minute and start talking to her heart."

"Woo?"

"Ah, boy. This is gonna take some additional help." Brock led the way to the rest of the crew gathered in the trailer eating lunch.

They stepped inside and the room grew quiet. *This can't be good.* Corbin took off his hard hat and tossed it to the side.

"Have you tried flowers?" The newest member of the team, and youngest at nineteen, spoke before the others.

Corbin narrowed a look toward Brock.

"A newlywed wears a goofy smile nonstop and rushes home every chance he gets. You don't do either. So don't blame me. You told them all by yourself."

"Don't sweat it, Boss, we've all been there. Just not this soon!" Another worker heckled. Others joined in.

Someone suggested candy and another, a fancy dinner.

"Those ideas have leverage if you're apologizing, but the Boss's case is special." Whiskers, a middle-aged man with the crew for three years, took the last bite of his sandwich. As he chewed he readjusted his ball cap, drawing attention to the five inches of hair sticking out beneath it. He turned toward the boss. "First, you have to earn her trust. *Prove* yourself."

Brock's eyes widened as he whispered. "Did you know that guy could talk?"

Corbin shook his head.

Whiskers stood and cupped the jaw of a seated worker. "You stare at her, first thing in the morning," he swung his hand toward the other men, as if they all, but Corbin, knew what the next step was, "and tell her how beautiful she is."

Laughter erupted around the table. Several batted their lashes in fun while one thanked him in a high pitched voice.

Encouraged, Whiskers continued his act and picked up a wrapper that had fallen to the floor. "Help her around the house without being asked."

Corbin leaned toward Brock. "He's not going to break out in song, is he?"

"Let's hope not," Brock's deep voice answered.

Whiskers ran his hand through a tuft of hair sticking out above his ear. "Tuck a strand of hair behind her ear ... and whisper ..." He trailed off in a fluent line of Spanish.

Corbin had no idea the man could speak English, let alone another language, nor what he'd said, but he caught the gist. They all expected him to do the same thing Jessie wanted ... show her affection.

Wasn't there another way?

Chapter Eleven

Corbin pulled into his drive fifteen minutes ahead of the school bus. With the shelter open for overnight accommodations, they expected Jessie's Thursdays to lengthen dramatically.

Like each day since marrying Jessie, he opened the door to a clean, freshly scented home. The kitchen counters were free of clutter and wiped down. Throw pillows neatly arranged on the couch. Each room he paced through showed evidence of Jessie's giving nature. The children's laundry folded on their beds, and left for them to put away. When did she have time for the wash? Perhaps she ran the laundry the day before then folded them this morning.

Inside their bedroom Corbin stared at his open closet. While his clothes had all been put away, it appeared she ran out of time to fold her own.

He scooped up the pile of shirts and jeans and dropped them on the bed. He mused over the intimacy of folding the clothes of a woman he hadn't even kissed. A picture of her cut and bruised mouth at the wedding came to mind. That kiss didn't count. Afraid he might hurt her, he'd barely touched her lips.

The school bus brakes screeched as he put away the last of her clothes. He met the children at the door in a clobber of hugs. Layla fastened herself onto his leg, forcing him to drag his foot with each step.

"We're hungry." The boys yelled.

"Then let's cook supper."

Shannon tugged his arm. "Dad, do you think that's a good idea?" We could wait for Mom. She doesn't burn stuff."

"I don't burn *everything*."

She stopped and pointed. "You don't want to mess up the clean stove though do you?"

Corbin admired the smooth white surface, thanks to Jessie. "No, I don't. So I guess you're cooking with me."

Despite his daughter's protests, Corbin opened the freezer, then the pantry, and perused the sparse shelves. "Looks like it's chili night. Then we'll go grocery shopping."

Corbin thawed the hamburger in the microwave while Shannon opened three cans of beans, all different varieties. She poured them into the crockpot as Corbin cooked the meat.

When it was stirred together he glanced down at Layla, still attached to his leg. "Okay, munchkin, tell the boys it's time to go."

"Without Mommy?"

"She'll be here before we leave." Though he didn't understand why, he knew when Jessie was near. Whether she stepped into the room before he had a chance to turn or he saw her in town, her presence triggered something inside him.

The garage door rolled up, signaling her arrival. "Wow, Daddy, you were right."

***

Corbin glanced at Jessie. She'd readily agreed to go shopping then offered her keys for him to drive. Though his truck had been enough for his two children, with four, the family needed a van.

Jessie buckled as he climbed behind the wheel like a normal married couple.

"Thank you for making chili." She smiled tentatively and readjusted her seat belt.

Corbin resisted the unexpected urge to squeeze her hand. Instead he reached for the tin of peppermints he'd stuck in her van and popped one in his mouth. "You're welcome. I figured your day would be pretty full. How'd it go?"

"Busy. We had a lot of new faces. Some families. One man came in to eat with his wife and kids then left them at the shelter. You could tell it was really hard on him. He kept touching her and rubbing her back and hugging his children." Jessie sniffed and glanced out the window.

For her sake, Corbin sought for a better subject. "What about the friend you made? The one whose husband works in the city."

"Heather? She came by. Again, it was close to the end of lunch."

"Did you drive her home?"

Jessie stiffened. "Yes, but Vera went with me. Heather's oldest two were in school so there was room."

Corbin recognized the stubbornness in Jessie. It always came before she did something foolhardy.

He was silent a moment before asking, "Would you still have if Vera couldn't go along?"

"No." She fidgeted with her hands. "You asked me not to, so I figured if it came to that Oscar could have followed or even offered to drive some of the kids in his Volkswagen. What kid wouldn't want to ride in Herbie?"

Her answer eased the tightness in his chest. "Smart girl." Although they hadn't had any trouble, they could. The volunteers worked in groups for safety. He directed the conversation back to Heather. "So how was she?"

"Still stressed. The little one had another cold."

"Is her husband home on the weekends?"

She stared at him. "I actually asked the same thing. Yes, he is. He's tried to get overtime but hasn't managed to yet."

"Good. We can run by this weekend. Maybe he'd be interested in working for me."

She turned her warm smile on him and touched his arm. "Thanks, Corbin."

He understood the softness in her heart toward the homeless. Although Pastor Wade first proposed the shelter, Corbin worked alongside him from the very beginning.

He stole a look at Jessie's hand before she pulled away. It felt so right when she touched him, but he wouldn't encourage it. Not until he was ready to give her more. It wouldn't be fair. He inwardly shrugged. At least that's what Brock suggested.

"By the way, if you don't have anything against it, I'd like to donate the furniture we stored in your garage to the shelter."

Corbin signaled at the intersection then glanced at her in amazement. "Are you sure? You don't want to sell it?" He wouldn't think less of her if she wanted to make a profit, still, he hoped for a different answer.

"I couldn't buy our kids Christmas gifts with money that could've helped another family. Not when the needs are right in front of me."

"I'm proud of you, Jess." He knew her antique business was suffering, and it bothered her she wasn't able to add to the family income, yet she was still willing to swallow pride to help others. His fondness toward her grew. God had blessed him in so many ways with his wife.

At the store, Jessie pulled out her list and headed for the produce aisle. She chose a bundle of bananas and handed them to a child beside her then selected apples. Corbin stood back and watched, enjoying the family scene.

Jessie reached forward and picked up an apple. Turning it over in her hand, she replaced it for another, all the while, keeping her bottom lip tucked beneath her teeth. He loved watching her concentrate.

On the toiletries aisle, Corbin grabbed a pack of mega toilet paper rolls while Jessie led Layla back toward the cart, the girl's little arms filled with paper towels.

Corbin emptied his into the cart. "By the way, when you change the paper at home, it should roll off from the top."

"Seriously?" Jessie's mouth quirked and her eyes narrowed.

"Y-e-s." He drew the word out. Why did he have a sinking feeling that despite the aggravation he'd dealt with every time she'd changed a roll he should've kept his mouth shut?

"I see. Because it's so aggravating when you're ready to use it and you don't know which way it's rolling from. I mean, there's *so* many choices. Is it going to come from the top or the bottom?" Her head slanted toward her shoulder as she gave a heavenward glance. "Real taxing."

Corbin loved her feistiness, but tried not to expose the humor she roused. "Okay, I deserved that." She rewarded him with one of her big smiles. His heart did a funny kind of dance. Could it be, with no regard to his best efforts, he was falling in … a deeper *appreciation* of her?

He followed the family to the next aisle and stared at the shelf beside him. This feeling couldn't be love. He didn't want to love her. Well love her, yes, like a friend, but not *fall* in love. He couldn't bear going through that again.

"Is it really that hard to make a decision?"

He jerked his chin over to Jessie then back to the shelf … of toilet bowl cleaners. He pulled his mouth to the side. "Well, we do have more people in the house."

"Ooh." She scrunched her face at his comment but wasn't fooled. "A penny for your thoughts."

His gaze dropped from the curiosity simmering in her brown eyes to the pretty form of her mouth. Brock's words of wisdom came back to him, *"Forget about her body and talk to her heart."* Corbin cleared his throat and glanced at their reckless boys tossing packaged sponges back and forth. Jessie caught the distraction and turned from Corbin to address the antics. He sighed with relief. For two days he'd managed to behave, but with Jessie's appeal, he didn't know how long he could hold out.

***

After loading the van with groceries, Jessie sat with the children while Corbin made a quick stop inside the local Christian bookstore before they closed. Through the large glass windows, she watched him hurry to the teen section then to the register.

Shannon tapped her arm. "Here's Dad's mints."

"Oh, I didn't know you had them." Jessie placed them in the storage compartment in front of the dash.

"Dad shares them with us." Shannon quieted a giggle from Layla and the boys.

Corbin waved to the store employee before pushing on the door. He tried again then looked over his shoulder. Jessie saw the owner laugh and shake his head before Corbin pulled the door open. Within moments, he was back inside the van.

"Too many choices?"

"No, I found what I wanted." He held up the store bag.

"I mean with the door. Do I push or pull?" she asked in a mocking voice. Then snickered, "Or maybe it rolls up from the bottom."

His eyes narrowed before he pulled his mouth in a sideways smile. He touched the tip of her nose. "And you're a comedian tonight."

Her skin zinged to life. "And you're improving."

He cocked a brow.

"You touched my nose."

"Is that how easy it works?"

"You'd be surprised."

Corbin's steady gaze sent a rivulet of excitement through her veins. Her palm suddenly itchy, Jessie rubbed it over her leg. Corbin followed the movement. Was he contemplating holding her hand?

"Can we go home yet, I'm hungry," Garret yelled from the back seat, inviting a chorus of agreement from the other children.

"Yep, that's where we're headed." Corbin slipped the gear in reverse. He asked for the mints. Jessie held it open and he tossed one past his lips. Within seconds, his mouth drew down at the corners as his eyes darted from side to side. A cackle sounded from the back followed by a ripple of laughter. Corbin hadn't driven out of the parking lot when his tongue crawled out from his mouth. He managed to say, "Wha' am I ea'in?"

Like a volcano, the children's laughter erupted. Although Jessie didn't know what over, their joy pulled her in until laughter bubbled from her chest, too. Corbin brought the van to a stop and removed the offending object from his tongue.

Jessie flipped on the dome light. "A rock?"

A humorous glint sparked in his eyes. "Don'th acth inna'cent." He wiped his tongue numerous times with his hand. "You're the funny one tonight."

Jessie tried to explain but could only manage inarticulate sounds.

Shannon piped up from behind him. "I was going to tell you before you put it all the way in your mouth." She snorted, "It was just a joke."

Corbin smacked his tongue on the roof of his mouth. "Limestone. Yum."

"I had no idea. I wasn't in on this one." Jessie caught her breath and offered him a bottle of water she kept in the door. "And may I point out, that was from *your* daughter."

"Hey," Shannon argued, "I'm yours too, now."

The smile Corbin turned on Jessie melted her heart. She wished he wasn't so easy to love. Pushy and bossy, yes, but still too easy to love.

***

Jessie turned to Corbin in bed and asked, "What did you buy at the book store?" With having to put away groceries and still eat dinner, the evening had swept by without a thought toward his purchase.

"A book for Shannon." Again, he lay facing her. He smiled and they both laughed at the memory of his daughter's scheme. "She's in a practical joking stage. My only concern is that the other three will pick it up, too."

When the funny memory passed, Corbin spoke again. "The book's about sharing your faith. It gives examples of arguments to make nonbelievers consider their own belief."

"Wow," Jessie marveled. She'd never given thought to the full potential of her neighbor. "That scores you high dad points."

Through the semidarkness of the room, his penetrating gaze held her in suspense as he seemed to contemplate his next words. "How am I doing on husband points?"

She detected a note of vulnerability in his husky voice. How did she answer? She'd already determined not to withhold from him, yet still wanted more. With her voice lighthearted, she answered, "You're showing improvement."

"Good." He snuggled deeper into his pillow and closed his eyes.

What? That was it? No more playful banter or …

She squinted to peer closer. His eyes remained closed. Jessie rolled onto her back and stared at the ceiling. She could ask him if he was asleep. They could talk a little more. Or she could run a finger over his jaw … though his hair. But is that what she really wanted? Honesty forced its way to the surface.

She released the breath she'd unknowingly held. Yes, she wanted to talk, because talk might lead to hand holding. Hand holding might lead to … no, she really wasn't ready for more than that. For intimacy to bless their marriage, it had to have roots. And pillow talk was a good place to start.

From the corner of her eye, she glanced back at Corbin. The man couldn't be asleep. He wasn't breathing deep enough yet. How could he lie there like there was nothing going on between them? As if to prove her wrong, a sleepy, relaxed sigh slipped from his lips.

Chapter Twelve

After working late into the night on Friday so the new owners could move into her house, Jessie and Corbin slept in Saturday morning.

Noise from the hallway drew Jessie from her dream. She blinked at the sunshine reflecting off the adjacent walls and threw an arm over her eyes. Her hand plonked against Corbin's forehead. In a quick reaction she drew back, but he didn't stir.

She eased onto her elbow and stared at the man sleeping beside her. Having awakened before dawn each morning since their wedding, she hadn't witnessed him in this light.

The covers lay rumpled halfway down his chest. One muscled arm hung off the bed along with his right foot. His other arm rested on top of the blankets, making it impossible to pull the covers up for him.

Though his short cropped hair was hardly mussed, his jaw already showed a heavy amount of dark stubble. She'd always thought of Corbin as handsome, but somehow, seeing him embraced in the comfort of sleep, made him more endearing.

Her gaze trailed his length again, appreciating the effects of his hard work.

Another sound came from the hall, signaling if she didn't get up soon, the kids would come to her. She swung back to take one more look at her sleeping husband, only to find his eyes fully opened.

A smirk pulled on his handsome mouth. "See anything you like?"

Jessie's eyes widened as she gasped, "Oh, please." She pushed against the mattress to rise when he caught her braid.

Corbin gave a gentle tug while still lying down. Jessie stilled and chanced another look. His eyes centered on her hair while his hand worked off the ponytail. Once freed, he ran his fingers though the braided sections, separating them. Not a word was spoken. Their eyes locked in an intense moment. Hardly aware of her movement, Jessie leaned forward as Corbin rose toward her.

"Good morning, Mom! Morning Dad!" The door slammed against the wall with Timmy's announcement. "This morning we're serving Shannon's chocolate chip pancakes, topped with cool whip and strawberries."

Jessie spun around and sat ramrod straight, her mind tried to accept what almost happened and still listen to her son. *Did he say Cool Whip?*

Shannon entered carrying a tray with Layla in tow. Garret, missing in action, only meant something else was going on.

"Yum, thanks, kids." Corbin pulled a shirt over his head before Shannon settled the tray on the bed.

"And Garret's bringing fresh coffee."

Jessie glanced beside her. The worry in Corbin's eyes meant he shared her concern.

Garret appeared in the doorway watching the cups he carried, and made his way toward them. "They're only filled halfway so I wouldn't spill them."

"That was smart." Corbin complimented his son as he reached for a cup.

"Shannon made me," Garret mumbled.

"That's because you'd already spilled some."

Jessie noticed a shiny gel on Garret's arm. "What's that?"

"Aloe Vera," he beamed. "I see Dad do it all the time when he burns himself."

Jessie raised a brow. "Is that why there isn't much left of that poor plant?"

Corbin smiled and said, "Don't judge. Obviously, the kids have learned an important lesson in first aid." He forked a big bite of pancakes.

"Maybe we should back up and teach some safety rules first." She enjoyed ribbing him as much as he seemed to enjoy the attention. Jessie glanced at Shannon who waited for her to take her first bite. Jessie closed her mouth around her fork as syrupy sweetness coated her tongue. "Umm, umm."

Shannon beamed and spun on her heel. "Come on, Layla, let's clean up now."

As soon as she turned, Jessie bit into a ball of baking powder that hadn't mixed up. Her eyes welled as her body shivered from the bitter surprise.

"Are you cold?" Corbin stopped chewing.

"No, just a bitter bite."

"Yeah, I've gotten a few of those, too." His smile broadened as he opened his mouth for another bite then spoke around his food. "They'll expect clean plates, but if you can't eat yours, I will for you."

The man could be so gracious and thoughtful. Wrapped in the warmth of the moment, Jessie started, "I—"

She cleared her throat in a quick save before uttering the words that would've wiped the smile from Corbin's face. He wasn't ready for her heart. She only wished she hadn't fallen so fast. "I ... can finish them. They're not so bad."

***

Jessie sucked her bottom lip to the side of her mouth and fingered a lock of hair that had escaped getting twisted in the towel. A sigh of pleasure slipped past as she thought of Corbin loosening her braid. He had feelings for her. But to get him to acknowledge the fact might take a little ingenuity.

The oil elixir always softened her hair and gave it a smooth shine. Corbin may never notice, but what would it hurt to try?

Jessie hung the towel back on the rack. She pumped the oil onto her palm then distributed it through her hair. If nothing else, it would protect her ends from the heat of the blow dryer. By the time she finished her morning maintenance, her softened hair shone from top to bottom.

"Wait, Mom." Garret blocked her path outside the bedroom. He held a remote control in his hand and seemed to be waiting for a signal from Timmy who was positioned in the living room.

Layla twirled in front of the T.V. dressed in her pink tutu. Timmy shifted around her to make his signal. His smile split from ear to ear as he eagerly nodded. Garret pushed a lever forward, then to the side, then forward again.

"How can you see where you're going?" And what was he driving?

"With the camera."

She looked over his shoulder and saw a miniature screen on the control. The camera it was wirelessly hooked to must have been mounted on top of a remote control car. The kitchen floor came into view, then the bottom cabinets. "Uh oh," Jessie mouthed. Someone's sock clad feet shuffled by in the kitchen. She immediately knew their target.

"Ow!"

Garret flung the control toward Jessie then raced into his room and closed the door.

"I told you, Garret—" Corbin's fast-moving frame came to a sudden halt. "Jessie?"

"I didn't do it!"

"You're as bad as the kids." Even as he said the words, his attitude lightened. He reached for the controller and stared. "Did you do something different with your hair?"

Satisfaction oozed through her, but to avoid giving herself away, she simply shrugged. "I took care of it, is all."

She left the controller in his grasp and brushed by him toward the kitchen. She wasn't purposefully being a tease, but if she reacted to her onslaught of feelings, Corbin wouldn't be able to handle them. It was best to reel him in like a catfish. Long. Slow. Tugs.

"Is that for me?" Jessie pointed to one of the cups of steaming coffee on the table.

"Yes." Corbin pulled out a chair for himself and removed his sock.

Jessie stared at his ugly, purple and black toenail. "Ooh, what happened?"

He tilted his head and squinted. "You don't remember?"

She shook her head.

"I didn't want to work without my steel-toed boots and you said, and I quote, 'You're just fixing a spot in the floor not building a mall.'" He raised his voice several octaves to imitate Jessie's.

Jessie gasped and pointed to his foot. "That's from dropping a piece of wood?" The nail would likely fall off. She covered her mouth to hide the giggle that tumbled out. "I'm sorry. It's really ugly. Does it hurt?"

He looked at her from lowered brows, as if to say, *do you really have to ask*. He snatched the controller from the table and shoved it on top of the cabinets. "Thanks to Garret's practical joke, my toe's throbbing."

At least he couldn't blame it on her kids.

She paused. Shannon and Garret referred to her as mom without hesitation. She needed to return the full acceptance, because now they were all her kids.

An hour before noon, Jessie directed Corbin to the motel door she thought was Heather's. Paper and soggy boxes littered the sidewalk running beneath the eave. Corbin parked beside an older version of her van, directly in front of the room.

"You kids stay seated and we'll see if they want to go out to eat with us." She stepped onto a scattering of cigarette butts.

Together, she and Corbin waited for their knock to be answered. A television turned down. A man, equal in size to Corbin, sporting a goatee on his chin and a child in his arms, opened the door.

"Can I help you?"

Jessie peered around him and waved to one of the boys. He smiled and ran past his dad and wrapped his arms around her waist.

"Whoa, son." The man grabbed the boy's shoulder.

Heather came to the door and smiled. "It's okay, this is the woman I told you about from the shelter."

The man's gaze dropped to the ground. "Oh, hi," he mumbled. His pride took a sizeable hit.

Corbin cleared his throat. "Jessie tells me you work construction."

The man looked up again, his facial features wrapped in curiosity.

"I run a crew here in town and could always use another good man. How about you and your family join us for lunch and see what we can work out?"

"Dale?" Heather's pleading gaze begged her husband.

Soon they took seats at a long table in Smokey's Diner. "They have a good kids' menu." Jessie spoke to Heather while snapping her fingers at Timmy and Garret for them to settle down.

"Are they twins?"

"Yes and no. Corbin and I just got married, so now they're brothers who happen to be the same age."

Her new friend looked from Corbin back to Jessie. "Congratulations."

"Thanks." Corbin answered and put his arm around the back of Jessie's chair. His thumb raked across her shoulder. Little-by-little, the man was making progress.

A waitress passed their table carrying a tray of burgers and fries. The scent of grilled meat wafted through the air. Jessie's stomach rumbled in response.

"That's what I want!" cried one of Heather's boys.

"I want Tara noodles!" Layla beamed.

Heather scrunched her face in amusement and looked to Jessie for an explanation.

"She means macaroni and cheese. My friend Tara fixes that when we visit."

Their laughter linked the promise of friendship. Jessie enjoyed the excitement of getting to know new people. She loved to learn what made them tick, formed their personalities, and what their gifts were.

The toddler squirmed in Heather's arms.

"Can I take him?" Shannon asked.

"Here you go. Watch out he doesn't spill your water."

Shannon bounced the boy on her lap and let him play with her necklace. Layla scooted closer and baby talked to him. The child wouldn't lack for attention with those two around.

The men's conversation caught Jessie's interest.

"My contract doesn't end until the first of December. But after that, yeah, working here in town would be an answer to prayer."

Heather's shoulders visibly relaxed. "With all that we'd save on gas, maybe we could move into an apartment soon."

Corbin looked from her to Dale. "You knew the shelter opened up overnight housing, didn't you?"

The couple shared a look with each other. Heather cleared her throat. "We talked about it and … well, we've gone that route before. And no offense to your shelter, but between bedbugs and our things being stolen, we think it's best if we just stay where we're at."

A cloud of disappointment hung over Jessie. Didn't they know the shelter was new, at least the accommodations? Not to mention how quickly they could save toward their first and last month's rent needed to secure an apartment. "Would you please reconsider? The rooms are filling fast."

Corbin's thigh pressed against hers beneath the table. What had she done wrong? She only wanted the best for them.

Dale shifted in his chair and the reason was clear. He wasn't used to accepting help. This family was different from several who came through the shelter. Dale continued to work, even through their homelessness. It was evident taking care of his family was a high priority and not one he easily shared with others.

***

The rest of the day passed with Dale and Heather always in the forefront of Jessie's thoughts. The image of them at the restaurant, often touching with a brush of the hand or nudge of a shoulder. Even through all their trials, they pulled together. She and Corbin could learn a lot from them.

Jessie turned to Corbin in bed. Too tired for pillow talk, but she didn't want to risk a setback. She tucked her hand under the edge of her pillow, again, near Corbin's hand.

From the dim nightlight in the bathroom, she saw him smile, but he appeared more sad than happy. Was he also thinking of their new friends?

His gaze went from her face to her hand. "I still can't give you want you want, Jessie."

She closed her eyes, but couldn't block the hurt of his words. "Why did you have to bring that up?" She wanted to flip his forehead with her fingers. *Think before you speak!*

He flexed his jaw as his eyes grew intense. *Duh. Because he's a man and wants more than pillow talk.*

A river of tears swelled against her lids. Would he ever catch on? She rolled on her back to hide her emotions. A tear escaped and slid down her temple. She brushed it away. *God, not now. Don't make me go there. I'm not ready. Nor is he.*

Chapter Thirteen

Jessie reached for the phone beside the bed and glanced at the clock. Only a minute before the alarm was set to go off. "Hello." She turned her head away from the receiver to yawn.

"Good morning, Jessie. This is Corbin's mother, Sherry."

Jessie sat up, fully alert.

Corbin frowned. "Who is it?"

She mouthed, "Your mother."

"Good. She's been eager to talk to you but hadn't caught you at home." Corbin moved toward the bathroom. "Tell her hi for me."

Jessie stared at her retreating husband's back. A myriad of thoughts collided all at once. First, he was too good looking. Second, she was still mad at his comment from last night. And third, she knew Sherry, and thought the world of the woman, but hadn't addressed her as mother-in-law. A nervous anticipation thrummed through her veins. "Uh, Corbin says hi."

"I'm so happy to have you in the family, dear. I guess you know the reason we couldn't make the wedding, the short notice didn't give us time."

"Tell me about it."

Laughter bubbled across the line. "Oh, I'm sure it was a wise decision." She continued in small talk for a couple of minutes. Then asked, "Tell me, did you find plenty of space in the kitchen for your dishes?"

Jessie paused at the peculiar question. "Yes. There was lots of space."

"That's because after Beth died, Corbin had a bit of a tantrum. The kids were with me one day and he broke nearly everything he could in that kitchen. He'd never really dealt with death before. I guess he didn't know how."

"Oh."

"He has a delicate heart. Please take good care of it."

I would if he'd let me near it.

Sherry mentioned visiting at Christmas and said good-bye.

Jessie shuffled to the kitchen in a bit of a daze. Near the door, she found several nicks in the wall. They'd been dabbed over with similar paint. Now she understood where they came from.

As Jessie whipped up a batch of chocolate-chip muffins, she considered Corbin's fear. Although she sympathized with him, she wouldn't excuse his decision. The man had children. That didn't stop him from loving them … or her children. Somehow he needed to see he wasn't protecting himself. He was only making his life, and hers, very lonely.

She left breakfast to bake and read over the Sunday school lesson. At the end of the second page she paused. *What is this about?* With a sigh, Jessie turned back to the beginning and reread.

Half an hour later, she turned off the annoying timer on the stove and opened the oven door. A blast of heat warmed her face and riddled her cold arms with goose bumps. As chilly as the house felt this morning, the temperature must have dropped dramatically overnight. She would've never kept up with the electric bill had she moved to town. She set the muffin tins on the stovetop then opened the refrigerator to retrieve the milk.

"Yeah! It snowed!" Layla's eager cry carried from the living room.

"Really?" Jessie joined her at the window. "No, sweetie, that's just a heavy frost."

"No, it's ice." Corbin's voice startled her as he spoke from behind.

Jessie looked out the window again. It still looked like frost to her, but she'd keep her opinion to herself. She glanced at the clock. "It's almost time to go. Kids, eat some breakfast."

While the children clamored around the table, Jessie hurried off to the bedroom. Did every mother feel harried on Sunday morning? Between getting the kids up, making sure they were dressed appropriately and fed, she had little time to prepare.

She grabbed a brown sweater and her black skirt. The chilly temperature gave her the perfect excuse to wear the faux leather boots Tara had given her last year. She'd supposedly found them at a yard sale, but they didn't show any wear. Jessie pulled the zipper up her calf. The boots fit like a glove.

Corbin was already ushering the kids into the van by the time Jessie grabbed a muffin off the table. She noticed Corbin's black and red plaid wool jacket, similar in color to one of her favorite shirts. "I like your coat."

"I know. You tell me every year." He moved closer and buttoned her's.

The intimate act would've been welcomed if not for last night. Now it only added to Jessie's confusion. If he didn't want to love her, why did he show it through small acts of affection like this?

"I've had this coat since I was in high school. It was my Grandpa's." Corbin finished and moved back. His brow creased as he looked from Jessie's coat to his. "And despite the age, I think mine has held up better than yours. You need a new one."

Jessie was well aware of the fact. She wasn't sure what type of material her coat was made of, but it wasn't warm. However, money had been an issue for several years. "It's fine."

Corbin's chin dropped as he looked at her feet. "Well those boots sure aren't. They're a bad idea in this weather."

"No they're not." Jessie brushed a couple crumbs from her mouth. His sudden outpouring of attention made her uncomfortable. If he kept this up, they'd be late for church. "They'll keep me warm."

His gaze remained on her pointy heels as a sigh followed. "Ready?"

Corbin backed out of the garage and into the street.

"Wait a minute, I forgot my Bible." Jessie searched her purse for the house keys.

"Let me back up in the drive again and you can go through the garage."

"It's on the coffee table. I'll just open the front door."

Jessie exited the van and swung the door closed. The sharp movement, coupled with the slick ground challenged her stability. She wavered before regaining her balance. Corbin had been right, a thin sheet of ice layered the ground. She resisted looking his direction and carefully chose her footing across the lawn.

On the way back, Corbin stood in the yard. "I don't trust those shoes." He held his hand out for hers.

Aggravation toward his overcorrecting attitude gave way to bemusement. *He willingly offered his hand?*

Focused on him, Jessie forgot about the slippery surface beneath her. She reached forward as her foot slipped. Corbin caught her hand and tugged. She bumped into his chest before falling back and dropping her Bible. His arm slipped around her back.

Jessie swallowed a deep breath as she came to a halt over his thigh. Thanks to Corbin's quick lunge, she hadn't hit the ground. One hand clung to the back of his shoulder while the other rested against his chest. She pressed against him to right herself and their eyes locked.

Could he feel the pull between them? It was definitely more than attraction. Jessie's heart sped up as hope swelled like a brook in spring rains.

Corbin cleared his throat. "I knew you should've worn sensible shoes. You're going to break your neck in those."

145

Jessie straightened to her full height, plus heels. "You ruin every opportunity."

"What opportunity?"

"Exactly!" She picked up her Bible and stomped to the van. With her heels jamming through the icy layer on the lawn, she wouldn't fall. Unfortunately, her shoes would be scarred.

They drove to church in silence. After they signed the children into their classes, Jessie sought a momentary escape in the bathroom. Alyssa stood in front of the mirror, smoothing her hair. Jessie smiled to be polite when inside her guard went on full alert. Alyssa didn't respond.

Behind a closed stall, Jessie tried to pray, but the image of Alyssa kept interfering. *I don't know what I'm doing, Lord. I don't even know what to pray. Please let the Holy Spirit intercede for me.*

She walked out of the ladies room and into Corbin and Alyssa's conversation.

"It's definitely ice. Jessie almost found out the hard way."

Alyssa's hand pressed against Corbin's folded arms as she leaned forward, said something, then laughed in a false cheery tone. Corbin shrugged. Alyssa tilted her head in a pathetic look and motioned over Corbin's shoulder, "And there she is."

Jessie's competition strutted off with her shoulders pinned back and her back arched like a cat. *God, grab hold of that girl before I do.*

"Let's go." Corbin motioned forward.

Jessie didn't answer nor look his way.

Before they entered the sanctuary, Corbin stopped. "Shake it off, Jess."

"Which part?" Her jaw ached she clenched it so hard. "Everything you've said to me up 'til now, or everything *Alyssa* said to you?"

***

Pastor Wade's message drew to a close. He asked the pianist and soloist to come forward.

From the corner of her vision, Jessie watched Corbin's reaction as Alyssa passed their pew. Instead he turned toward Jessie. She quickly diverted her eyes then chanced a peek back. His face looked as if it had been carved in stone.

Jessie fingered the edge of her Bible, taking comfort from the feel of the thin paper as it flipped against her skin. The music started and she turned around once more to look for Heather and her family. They'd invited them. Had they come? Corbin sighed and she knew he didn't approve of her restless behavior. "They're here," she whispered.

"Who's here?"

"Heather and Dale."

He craned his head to follow hers then brought his hand up in a small wave before turning back around. "That's great." His eyes shone from genuine happiness. "Our efforts paid off."

The man might be thick when it came to personal matters, but his heart was pure gold toward the suffering of others.

If only he could see the suffering he caused her.

After church, Jessie hurried outside with the kids to catch up with Heather's family. Since no one had

147

been expecting the frosty layer, the parking lot hadn't been cleared. Without a grassy layer to dig her heels into, Jessie stepped carefully across the pavement.

The boys ran a few steps, then used their feet like ice skates to slide further. Layla tried to copy their antics. Just as Jessie warned her not to, she slipped and fell forward. Jessie lunged toward her and grabbed Layla's coat. Her boots twisted and spun her in a semicircle. In a blur of movement, she pulled Layla to her feet as she slid in her place. Jessie reached her hand out to break her fall but crumbled against her wrist.

Splayed on her side, with her hand twisted beneath her, pain throbbed through her arm.

***

After waiting three hours, they'd finally taken Jessie back. Corbin paced the emergency waiting room while the kids craned their heads to watch the television high in the corner. He'd be surprised if they left without complaints of their necks hurting. He chewed off another nail. Three already burned from tearing them to the quick.

He considered what Jessie had said when the children were away at the vending machine.

"You should've married Alyssa."

Corbin had blinked hard and stared at her wondering if he'd heard right. "What are you talking about?"

"She probably would've been easier to love."

Aggravated, he'd sighed and ran a hand over his face. "No, not at all. I don't have *any* feelings for her. Period."

Jessie cocked her head, "So you do have feelings for me?" She'd left a pause then added, "And if not, then all you did was marry me for convenience."

Trapped.

The children had returned then, ending the conversation.

Corbin stopped pacing and stared at the parking lot through a large window. What happened? They'd seemed closer before marriage.

He rubbed a hand over his chest. Her current absence left a gaping hole in his heart and guilt filled it. And rightly so. Was she right—had he only married Jessie for convenience? He'd argued the idea was preposterous, yet still couldn't shake the nagging feeling.

His temples throbbed with truths and possibilities he didn't want to face. But something had to change.

The children laughed and he turned to see. Caught up in the antics of Tom and Jerry, they were able to put their worries aside. He wished he could do the same.

"Corbin Vaughn." A nurse stood in the open doorway where Jessie had earlier disappeared. "The doctor would like to speak to you."

Corbin addressed the kids. "Stay together. Shannon's in charge." He stepped through the door, and the nurse smiled as if to calm his frayed nerves. Hospitals always made him uneasy. They reminded him of times he'd rather forget.

"She's right in here." The nurse held back a curtain separating the rooms enough to allow

Corbin to enter. "The doctor will be with you in a moment."

A slow, wide smile stretched across Jessie's face. She held up her arm. "Wanna sign my sh'ling?"

"What did they give you?"

"OxyContin." A man in a white lab coat entered. "I'm Dr. Howard. Your wife is more sensitive to the pain medicine than most. I think after her dose wears off, you'll be safe to give her an over the counter pain medication."

Jessie giggled and whispered loudly, "He looks like a mad scientist."

Corbin brushed her hair back from her forehead and put a finger to his lips to signal for her to be quiet. Though in reality, her goofy state relaxed him. He rested his hand on her shoulder and turned his attention to the doctor.

"The good news is Jessie didn't break her wrist."

"Yeah." Jessie clapped her good hand against the bed.

Dr. Howard smiled and shook his head. "Is she always this entertaining?"

"No—"

"Hmmm."

"I mean she is, but in a different way." A fuzzy feeling wrapped itself around Corbin's heart. He always found Jessie entertaining. Whether she was riled up defending her point of view, or just laughing at the antics of their family, he enjoyed being with her.

"Regardless, there isn't anything to worry about. Now back to her wrist." Dr. Howard pointed to an x-ray lit up on the wall. "Though it's not broken there are two tiny tears in her ligament. This type of moderate sprain can take anywhere from a week to ten days to feel back to normal, though it may take longer than that to heal completely. She said she doesn't do any sports, and since it's her left hand, she'll probably heal faster. I've written out my recommendations. Make sure she wears the splint to keep her arm elevated and ice it alternatively the rest of the evening."

Once the doctor finished, Corbin guided Jessie back to the waiting room. The children jumped from their seats and hurried to her side.

"Aw, Mom, I was hoping you would have a cast."

"I know." Jessie's bottom lip puckered out. "I wanted everyone to sign it. Instead, you can sign my sh'ling!"

Shannon's brow wrinkled. "Is Mom okay?"

"She's a little loopy from the pain medicine, but she'll be fine soon enough."

***

At home, the children each grabbed an apple for a snack then vanished to the living room where Jessie rested on the couch. Corbin didn't know who'd be more entertaining, the children or Jessie on OxyContin. She'd laughed, seemingly at nothing, all the way home.

Corbin stood at the stove cutting the partially frozen hamburger with his spatula. What if Jessie had hit her head? Images of his first wife, weak and pale, stabbed his heart. The disease that robbed her life had first stolen her strength and balance. He couldn't count the times she tried to do something on her own and fell.

Didn't Jessie understand? Probably not. Not only had they not known one another when his wife was alive, but her husband had died in a car accident. He hadn't suffered month after month. She didn't have the painful past of watching someone she loved, slowly lose their vitality.

"What's burning?" Layla's sweet voice intruded on his unwanted thoughts.

Startled, Corbin flicked hamburger off the spatula, disturbing the clean white ceramic top with bits of red meat. He refocused and scraped the skillet, freeing the burned layer of their taco dinner.

"Nothing. Dinner's almost ready."

Layla didn't leave. Big, blue eyes blinked up at him. Without warning, she closed the distance between them and wrapped her arms, and sticky apple, around Corbin's waist. "T'anks for saving Mommy."

Emotion clogged his throat. He moved the skillet off the burner and squatted eye level with Layla. "You don't have to thank me. I'd do anything for your Momma."

Her little arms slipped around his neck and tightened. "I love you."

He returned her hug. "I love you, too."

A voice inside seemed to sing, *and that's how easy it is.*

Chapter Fourteen

With the children in bed, Corbin flipped off the hall light and returned to the living room to check on Jessie. Propped up with pillows, she reclined with her eyes closed along the length of the couch. He smiled at his dark-haired angel. Even sleep couldn't hide her peppery spirit. Jessie's lids creased and her lips puckered. If he didn't know better, he'd bet she was dreaming of a smart retort to use on him.

He scooped up her legs and sat down, resting her ankles across his lap. He rubbed her feet and mentally revisited her fall. Though most of Jessie's near accidents were from carelessness, this one wasn't. She'd risked her own safety for her daughter's. He couldn't exactly fault her ... except for choice of footwear.

Corbin had already written down Jessie's shoe size and hoped to get away at lunch tomorrow to buy her something more sensible. Though she hadn't mentioned needing anything, from helping with her bills, he knew she hadn't the extra to spend on herself for quite a while.

An airy laugh slipped from Jessie's lips. Her toes wiggled as she squirmed. Corbin's hands stilled and so did she. When he resumed rubbing her feet, she again laughed in her sleep. Evidently, his wife had ticklish soles.

He glanced at his watch. Though it wasn't yet bedtime, today's haphazard events zapped him. Did he carry Jessie to bed like the last time she fell asleep on the couch, or leave her be?

With the pillows behind her, Jessie's arm would stay more elevated.

Corbin stared at her sleeping form. He didn't want to go to bed without her.

He reached for a quilt kept rolled on the floor between the couch and end table and covered them both. With his feet on the foot stool, he sunk back against the cushion, content to stay with his wife.

***

Corbin instructed a crewman where to drop-off the truckload of drywall. As soon as the man left, Brock appeared.

"I heard Jessie took a fall yesterday."

Corbin motioned to the driver of the truck to keep backing up. "Yeah. She sprained her wrist." He held his hand up and yelled, "That's good," then returned his focus to Brock.

"How are you dealing with that?"

Corbin and Brock had years of history. Brock knew about Corbin's struggles after losing Beth.

Corbin's jaw tightened. "How do you think? Every time I leave her side, I'm afraid she's going to … it's just like with Beth—only Jessie isn't sick."

Gnawing worry churned in his gut. He'd called home before lunch and wanted to again.

"Did you know the phrase *fear not* is used over a hundred times in the Bible?"

Corbin clenched the clipboard in his hand. Brock only meant to help, but he didn't have a clue what Corbin was dealing with. "And sometimes it's easier to read than apply."

He stomped toward his truck before Brock could tell him he lacked faith. He yanked the passenger door open and stared at the blueprints but saw nothing. With the worsening weather, two men calling in sick this week, and the Thanksgiving holiday, his tight schedule was falling apart … not to mention life at home.

"God," Corbin bowed his head where he stood, "I'm not doing too good on my own." A cold breeze whistled through the cab, instantly pulling his thoughts back to work and the schedule that kept slipping from his grasp. His first instinct was to study the blueprint again, count the men he had available and consider hiring more. He fought off the urge and leaned an elbow on the seat with his temple resting between his thumb and middle finger. *Help me block everything else out so I can hear you, God. Tell me what I'm to do.*

A few impatient moments later, Corbin sensed the same thing he already knew. Leave worries in God's hands. But falling behind on this job meant the next project would start behind schedule.

What's wrong with that?

Whether it was his own seeking conscience or the Spirit, the question needed an answer.

"My reputation," Corbin whispered. His lips tightened in self-disapproval. Caught up in the rat race of life, he'd put his focus more on the world and its approval than on God.

A quick reflection of his problems only supported the fact. The reason for his stress? Relying on his own strength. He couldn't remember praying about the delay. He'd tried to handle it on his own.

And the same thing could be said for his marriage. Because of *his* past, *his* pain, he'd justified withholding love, but maybe it wasn't working. *If I'm wrong there, God, you'll have to show me. Cause I certainly don't want to go down that road again. I've been through enough.*

Saying the short prayer didn't lighten his burden. Maybe because it wasn't really formed as a prayer and deep in his heart he knew he still wasn't relying on God.

***

Jessie leaned toward the mirror and studied a tuft of hair. With her other hand too sore to use her fingers, there was no way she could snip the split ends. She was way overdo for a cut.

The phone rang. A flutter tickled her abdomen. Could it be Corbin again? He'd called two hours ago to check on how she was feeling. His thoughtfulness touched her heart. If only he knew how easy it was for her to love him. *Please, God, open his eyes soon. I'm tired of holding back.*

She picked up the cordless and moved to the couch. "Hello."

"How you feeling?" Tara's voice held a tender tone. "Corbin swept you away before I had a chance to see how bad you were hurt."

Jessie almost laughed at Tara's choice of words. No one really knew how swept away she was. But she couldn't reveal her heart, least of all to Corbin, not when he didn't want it.

It was so much easier when she stayed aggravated at him.

"The doc says I just sprained my wrist. All I know is it really hurts and the over-the-counter pain medication isn't helping." A moan escaped as she repositioned herself on the cushions.

"Can't they give you something stronger?"

"They did and Corbin and the kids are still having fun over my reaction." Jessie tucked the phone in her shoulder and reached for the quilt on the couch. She woke up before dawn, her leg feeling prickly as a cactus. Corbin slept with his head resting on her thigh.

"Jessie, where'd you go?"

"Huh? Sorry, I was thinking about something."

"I said I'm glad I caught you at home. Justin surprised me and took the week off. We're going to get away from family and away from stress."

"Wow, that's nice. It's also nice to know you don't file those under the same thing."

Tara snorted. "Yeah, isn't it?"

She sounded better than she had a week ago. Maybe this trip would be what Tara and Justin needed. Jessie ran a hand over her head and her thoughts turned selfish. Now who was going to wash and trim her hair? The trim could wait, but she definitely couldn't wait a week for the other.

***

The bus pulled away as the children piled through the door. The room seemed to shrink with their voices. They all wanted to know how she was and to share the events of their day.

After the rush of greetings ended, Shannon settled on the couch next to Jessie while Layla sat at her feet and dumped her backpack. "Are you fixing dinner tonight or do we have to eat what Dad makes?"

"I prepared lasagna. All that's left is to put it in the oven."

"How'd you do that with one hand?" Shannon peered at Jessie's fingers extending from the sling.

"Don't worry. I didn't use this one." Though the dish had been more difficult than she'd considered, she'd managed by pulling the noodles out of the pan with tongs instead of draining the water.

The garage door rumbled from the other side of the living room wall. Jessie looked at the girls in surprise. "Your dad's home already?"

"Yeah! He can play donkey." Layla scrambled to her feet, scattering papers and pencils as she ran to the kitchen.

"Hi, Munchkin."

Long before they were married, Jessie always anticipated the sound of Corbin's voice each afternoon. No matter the day he had, he seemed to leave his troubles behind when addressing the children.

He rounded the corner with Layla trying to scramble onto his back.

"Play donkey."

"No, not now. We have to help your momma." His eyes locked onto Jessie. "How you feeling?"

"I'm fine." All but her wrist. A wave of pain washed over her with the slightest movement. She almost wished they would've set her arm in a cast. "You're home early."

His face softened as he watched her stand and cross the floor. Corbin rubbed the side of her arm. "Does it feel any better?"

Jessie swallowed, but couldn't quite clear the response of his touch from her voice. "Not yet, but it'll get there."

"Where'd the boys go?" Shannon's sudden curiosity also drew Jessie's attention.

"I saw them come through the door. They must be in their room." *What kind of mischief were they into now?*

Corbin strolled down the hall. "Guys?" He knocked but didn't get an answer. He pushed the door open. A stream of Nerf bullets flew from the room, pinging off Corbin and the wall.

A bubble of happiness erupted from Jessie's chest in a roll of laughter. Though their children were always up to something, their harmless fun never made more than a little mess.

Despite their tumultuous start, she'd laughed more since marrying Corbin than she had in a long time.

The girls quickly joined sides against the boys.

From the window, she caught a dot across the street. An orange-striped cat slowed as he reached the yard. He flicked water from each foot as he stepped across the lawn. The weather had warmed enough to melt the mess it left yesterday.

Unaware of being watched, the feline stopped below the front window and pawed the flower bed. "Oh, great. This is where you choose to do your business?"

Jessie opened the front door. "Scat!" The cat scrambled off toward Mrs. Clarkson's.

The neighbor's front door opened, and out came the very reason for the over population of cats in the neighborhood.

"Mrs. Clarkson," Jessie walked onto the front porch in her house shoes.

"Oh, hello-o!" Mrs. Clarkson waved as she continued toward the side of the road with her bowl of garbage.

"Please, would you mind not dumping that there? I nearly ran over a cat the other night."

"And how are you enjoying being married, dear?"

Jessie pressed her lips tight. Like always before, whenever Mrs. Clarkson refused to give a direct answer, she would change the subject as if she hadn't heard the question.

"We're doing well, but please stop dumping your garbage in the street."

"Oh, I'd never do a thing like that." She emptied her pail and tapped the bottom to insure all its contents were gone. "*Tsk. Tsk.* Cars would drive over it and make quite the mess. That's why I dump my gardyloo on the side where the drain can wash away the waste."

Jessie took a deep breath. Why did this woman have to be so difficult? Gardyloo or garbage, did she really think the gutter of the road was any better? She'd try to persuade her from a different point of view.

"But dumping it on the side of the road endangers those cats you love. They run out in front of vehicles and like you, I don't want them getting hurt." Not to mention she didn't want the foul odor and fly infestation the garbage would create come summer.

"You're right, dear." Mrs. Clarkson hugged the pail to her middle and paused on her walkway as though giving the matter proper consideration. "Thank you so much for telling me. I'll have to find another spot. Ta, ta, now." She smiled and waved.

***

The aroma of melting cheese and Italian spices drew everyone toward the kitchen. The children helped set the table while Corbin removed the lasagna from the oven. Jessie tossed the salad with one spoon and watched him work. Having a man in the kitchen was a new experience. Richard had always joked he'd die of starvation if she ever left him.

Corbin sliced another piece of French bread as if he'd done it a hundred times. Each piece an equal thickness to the first. It felt good sharing the responsibility. Almost intimate.

After dinner, Shannon helped clear the table and put away food, then ran off to play with Layla. Jessie discovered one of Shannon's pet peeves. She couldn't stand touching food left on plates, including her own. Nothing a pair of rubber gloves wouldn't solve in time.

Jessie ran hot water and dish soap in the sink on top of the dirty pans.

"You're cooking's going to ruin me." Corbin patted his stomach as if he had reason for concern.

An image of Corbin changing shirts after playing with the kids popped into Jessie's head. From where she stood, he didn't have anything to worry about.

"See something you like?"

She drew her eyes up to meet his teasing gaze. How could she have allowed herself to get caught? "You seem to like that phrase, but I wasn't thinking about you," she playfully answered back then swallowed, but it didn't solve the dryness in her throat. Pleasant relief lifted her shoulders. His teasing was back … she hoped for good.

Jessie reached to put the bowl they hadn't used back in the cabinet.

Corbin whispered over her shoulder. "White lies are the same as big ones."

Startled by his nearness, Jessie teetered on tip toes then lowered herself back down, her back brushing against Corbin's chest. His presence stole her breath. He slid to her side and slipped the wash cloth from her hand.

"I'll do the dishes."

Jessie studied his gaze. He wasn't closing himself off. Like the soap bubbles popping on top the water, hope exploded inside her. Something had changed.

A smile teased the corner of his mouth. If she didn't know better, he was enjoying her attention.

Nothing new there. What was new, was him giving back without expecting something physical in return.

He rinsed the plates and stacked them in the dishwasher. "How about after we get the sink cleaned, I wash your hair?"

Jessie blinked and dropped her mouth open. "Did Tara call you today?"

"No."

"Then how—"

"Unless you can wash it with one hand, I figured you'd need the help."

She cocked her head to the side. "You keep surprising me."

"Good."

For a quick moment, his eyes revealed a vulnerability she hadn't seen before. He was making progress. *What caused the change?* She brushed away the question. The reason mattered little when compared to the results. Jessie was willing to keep his pace, especially after his mother's revealing story. Although Jessie had mourned for Richard, and still did at times, she hadn't experienced Corbin's long struggle.

She looked around the kitchen. Did it still remind him of his first wife?

"Have you decided on a color?"

Jessie whipped her head back around. "I, uh ..." compassion filled her heart. She hadn't considered it before, but presumed he needed the change. "I saw a picture in a magazine somewhere of a retro kitchen. The walls were a beach blue and the cabinets white, like yours." The color scheme was a stretch and she didn't expect him to agree, but the idea blurted out.

Corbin copied her former action and glanced about the kitchen as though seeing it in the new color. "Let's do it."

"Really?" Jessie couldn't have controlled her smile if she'd wanted to. "When can we start?" She moved to clasp her hands together, forgetting about her wrist. A sharp stab reminded her of her current limitations. "Ow."

"Maybe after Christmas. You should be plenty well by then."

Later, with her head bent over the sink, Corbin adjusted the water until she said, "Good." She closed her eyes as his fingers kneaded her scalp through the rivulets of the sprayer. Tonight, he touched her more than he ever had. Jessie liked it. A lot.

"You have great hair."

His comment stilled her heart.

She pulled herself out of the dreamy state. "Richard always thought I should cut it. He said it was too unmanageable."

Corbin's chest pressed against her shoulder as he worked in the shampoo. His breath whispered against her ear. "He was wrong."

Chapter Fifteen

Corbin walked the perimeter of the new building, satisfied with the work his crew accomplished. If the weather cooperated, three and a half weeks from now he'd be enjoying Christmas with his family, completely at ease.

Since Jessie's fall, something had changed between them. Now he couldn't wait to get home, make sure she was okay, help with chores, and simply be with her.

He met his crew by the trailer and passed out their paychecks. "You guys have a happy Thanksgiving. Pray that any bad weather headed this way will hit this week instead of next."

"Wanting to be snowed in with the missus, are you?" Whiskers snickered. Some of the other men joined in.

"Actually, I wouldn't mind at all."

A manly cheer rose from amongst the crew. Several patted him on the back as they left for the week. When Corbin reached Whiskers, he stopped and asked, "How long have you been married?"

"Thirty-two years." The man's beard moved with his smile.

"Do you do those things you suggested last week?" Corbin had never asked personal questions of his crew unless someone fell into trouble. But now, curiosity wouldn't let him rest.

"Whatever it takes."

"To get out of trouble?"

Whiskers chuckled. "No. Whatever it takes to keep the fire lit." Crinkles formed at the corners of his eyes.

"Thanks. I think I'm beginning to catch on."

"Weren't you married before?"

Corbin braced himself for the pending questioning and brutal hazing men loved to dole out to others. "Yeah."

A man beside Whiskers frowned. "Then how did that work? Did she just keep her head down and do your bidding?"

Corbin blinked several times as his mind struggled to take him further back. Hurt by Beth's illness and death, he rarely thought of the years they had together. The memories were too painful.

An image of her laughing with the children slowly resurfaced. He saw the room she was in, often messy with the kids' toys. They argued over little things, but never anything big. Was it because she did everything he asked?

Brock cleared his throat from beside Corbin. "He and Beth had a good marriage. No, she didn't do his bidding."

Satisfied, the men took their checks and left, leaving the other two standing alone. Corbin turned to Brock. "Then what's different this time? And why is it taking me so long to catch on?"

"If you really want that answer, I'll give it to you."

Corbin followed him inside the trailer out of the blustery wind.

"You want to control things that are impossible." Brock poured two mugs full of steamy coffee and handed one to Corbin. "You can't prevent death. And only an idiot would keep himself from falling in love with his wife."

Corbin choked on his hot drink. He hadn't mentioned that to Brock, had he?

"It's the reason for all your issues, right?"

His jaw didn't clench. His hands didn't fist at his sides. Corbin wanted answers as well. With his throat tight, he managed a weak, "Yeah."

"Then start living the way God meant for you to."

***

Corbin rolled his sleeves up past his elbows. Jessie needed pies for the shelter tomorrow, and he'd offered to help out. Only, he'd never made a pie in his life.

"Put the apron on, Daddy." Layla held out Jessie's pink frilly apron.

"Where do you women get these things? Haven't I seen some at the shelter?"

Jessie smiled as he bent his head for Layla to don him with his new kitchen garment and answered, "A lady at church makes them."

He straightened, but before Layla could tie the back, tires screeched to a halt on the pavement outside.

They all turned toward the front of the house as Corbin hurried to the door and flung it open. An angry expression transformed the driver's face as she stared at their neighbor's house. When she caught sight of Corbin, the frown changed into a sputtering smile.

The driver rolled the window down and pulled even with their driveway. "Well, Mr. Vaughn. You're looking good ... if not pretty."

It was Mrs. Smith, who lived toward the end of the street. Corbin caught the ties of his apron as they flapped in the wind. The warmth of embarrassment tickled behind his ears. "Uh, thank you." In a need to explain, he continued talking, "I'm helping Jessie bake pies for the shelter."

"I dropped mine off this morning."

Although not all their neighbors attended the same church, they were good to pull together for the sake of their community.

Mrs. Smith's frown returned as she glanced back at Mrs. Clarkson's house. "Doesn't she know someone is going to run over those cats because of her garbage?"

"We've already talked to her about it. I'll try again."

As Mrs. Smith drove away, Corbin slipped his boots on. He glanced back at his family. "Kids, you help your mom get started, and I'll be right back."

He hurried across both lawns and knocked on the front door. Footsteps clipped on tile before the door opened just far enough to show Mrs. Clarkson's face. "Yes? Oh, Corbin, it's you." She welcomed him. "Come on in."

Corbin stepped through, thankful for the warm interior as he'd hurried over without his coat.

She pointed to a chair for him to sit. "Would you like some tea? It'll warm you more than that apron." A sly smile spread.

Corbin grunted. Why hadn't he thought to take it off? "No thank you, Mrs. Clarkson. I'm helping Jessie with pies so I can't stay long." He stared at the seat upholstered in flowers and lace then glanced at his apron. No sense worrying about his pride now.

He wriggled on the uncomfortable stiff cushion. "We need to discuss where you feed your cats."

"But I don't have any cats. I only offer scraps to the poor, little homeless animals." Her voice took on a coercing tone. "The same as you, offering care to those at the shelter."

"No, not the same at all. We offer folks a safe place to eat, we don't throw food out on the street for them." Corbin sighed. "Mrs. Clarkson, you promised Jessie you'd stop dumping your garbage in the road."

"Oh," she waved a hand, "that was just a terradiddle."

"A what?"

"A little lie." She dropped her chin and cocked her head in an impish antic. "I can't stop feeding them now. They depend on me."

Corbin rubbed a hand over his eyes. "Why can't you feed them in the backyard?"

"I might slip and fall. There's no footpath out back."

"Then hire someone to build you a walkway, but you have to stop dumping in the road. The cats will get run over or worse, you'll cause someone to wreck trying to avoid hitting them."

Mrs. Clarkson's eyes brightened and she brought a hand to her chest. "Oh. I just had a marvelous idea. You could do that for me. You build little things all the time, don't you? You could build me a cobble stone footpath and even a place to feed the helpless kitties."

Corbin was past clenching his jaw. He ground his teeth together until his head began to pound. There was no working with this woman. Conniving and manipulative, she was also belittling. Yet still, the only solution he could see was to build the silly sidewalk … and cat feeder.

Corbin said goodbye and returned to the house. All four kids looked up from the table with flour covered hands and faces. Jessie forced a smile. It was obvious her helpers weren't helping matters. "Okay kids, make room and I'll take over."

"Aw, Dad." Garrett wiped a floured hand over his forehead. "I almost have mine done."

Corbin glanced across the table at the pitted pie dough. One end was so thin he could see the table through it while the other was missing several sections that had stuck to the rolling pin. "I'll take it from here. Maybe you can mix the filling."

"No, I'm doing that." Shannon had a bowl beside her filled with an orange liquid about to slop over.

"Timmy, stop teasing me!" Layla's dough covered hands flew at her brother in anger.

"Stop." Jessie's commanding voice took control. "Go wash your hands, all of you but Shannon. We'll find something else for you to do."

Jessie pulled out a chair at the table and sat down. Her free hand pressed against her injured wrist.

"Does it still hurt?"

"Only when I move." A sheepish smile brushed away the stress from her features.

Contentment escaped on a sigh. "You're so pretty."

Jessie's eyebrows shot upward as her eyes widened. Corbin hadn't realized he'd complemented her out loud.

"Thank you," was her soft reply.

The unplanned, natural interaction put him at ease. Almost as if they had a normal relationship. *Help us get there, God. It's what we both want.* Like his last comment, the prayer was sent without prior thought. He was beginning to relax. Brock was right. Only an idiot would choose not to love his wife, especially when he was blessed with someone like Jessie, beautiful inside and out.

With the dough reshaped, Corbin concentrated on rolling it out evenly. Jessie instructed when to add more flour and helped rub down the rolling pin. She looked up at him. "You have flour on your nose. Right there." She touched a floured finger to the tip of his nose.

"The only thing saving you from my getting even is that sling. So milk it while you can."

She laughed at his threat while his mind imagined her without the injury, and the building possibilities. A desire to draw her to him and kiss her was only doused by Shannon sitting in the kitchen.

As if sensing the direction of his thoughts, Jessie moved to the end of the table and returned to the topic of their neighbor. "Did you get her to stop?"

Corbin set the rolling pin to the side. He couldn't talk about Mrs. Clarkson while working with dough or he'd have to start all over again. "Looks like I get to build her a walkway and a place to feed the cats."

"What?" Jessie's stern expression almost made him laugh, but he was smart enough not to. "She's afraid of falling in the backyard, and that's why she feeds them out front."

"That's bologna. She gets around fine."

"Do you see any other way around this? She ignores every citation and told me out right she lied when telling you she'd stop dumping it out front."

"Ooh, that woman!" Jessie thrummed her fingers against the table. "If you build her a place for the cats, you know they'll be in our yard all the time doing their business."

"I thought about that too, so I'll make a sand box for them."

"A sand box!" Layla had returned and looked up in excitement.

"Not for you." Jessie addressed their youngest. "You won't be able to play in this one. It's for Mrs. Clarkson's cats."

"Oh, they'll share. Cats are nice."

Shannon laughed. "You don't want to play in it, silly, it'll be their bathroom."

Layla's face pulled down in disgust. "G'oss."

Jessie tossed her hair behind her. "She probably expects you to do this for free, too."

He should've never mentioned the lie. It only made matters worse to his feisty little bride. He smiled as he watched her pace the kitchen and slam cabinet doors while pretending to look for something.

"I know!"

The search paid off. Jessie must've found a plan hidden in the cupboards. Corbin fought to keep his face serious and waited for her explanation.

"Let her hire Dale. He could use the extra work, especially over the holiday. And she'd have to pay him for material because he can't just go buy them."

Jessie's idea had merit. Dale would be stuck in the motel room with his family over the holiday and would probably love a reason to get out of the closed-in space and make extra money. "Are they coming to the shelter tomorrow?"

"Heather said they were. Let's talk to them then."

Her features brightened at the idea. Not only would she keep their neighbor from taking advantage of them, she'd also help out her new friend. Corbin couldn't resist, he pulled her toward him and kissed her hair where it met her forehead. "Good idea."

Her hand stilled where it had come to rest across his back. The air between them built with heat. Brock was right, he'd been an idiot. This woman had so much to give yet all he'd done was steal her happiness.

Not anymore.

***

Jessie scooped another slice of pie for the next visitor. A steady stream of folks lined up to eat at the shelter. If not for this food, where would they have eaten today? It was likely, most of them wouldn't have celebrated the holiday at all.

Nevin's lined face crinkled as he smiled. "How's my pretty girl today?"

"I'm great." Jessie's smile couldn't have stretched wider. "And happy to be here."

His eyes twinkled, "Come say hi to me when you get a chance."

The teenager Jessie saw last week moved up the line.

"Hi, it's nice to see you again."

The girl eyed Jessie as if measuring her honesty. "You remember me?"

"Of course. You sat down the table from Nevin."

"Who?"

"The man that was in front of you."

"Oh, yeah. I've met him before." She kept her head down and accepted a slice of pumpkin pie. "Don't expect me next time. I move around a lot."

The line moved forward, yet the girl's comment nagged at Jessie. She looked for an opportunity to slip away but there seemed to be no end. Did she really mean she planned on moving, or was she contemplating something else, like suicide?

Under different circumstances, Jessie probably wouldn't let her thoughts turn so dire, but she'd seen it happen before—and never wanted to again.

As if he could read her thoughts, Corbin motioned to her from a group of men he'd been standing with. He excused himself and squeezed into the busy kitchen. "Need a break?"

"Perfect timing. I want to talk to that teenager before she leaves."

"If it's the one I'm thinking of, she was hanging out by the door to the game room."

In preparation for today, Pastor Wade had suggested they set aside a room for the children. Vera and a few other women volunteers took turns staying with them.

As she drew near, the girl saw Jessie. The interest that glowed while the young lady watched the children in the room, transformed into a dull, you-bore-me kind of look. Jessie didn't care. Experience taught her it was a front, a protection of sorts.

"Was the food good?"

The girl shrugged. "It was okay."

Jessie sought to make small talk, but could only learn the girl called herself Sissy.

Layla saw Jessie and bounced across the room to give her a hug. "Hi, Mom." She turned to the teenager. "Hi. What's your name?"

Jessie introduced her, "Honey, this is Sissy."

Layla laughed. "Like my sissy, Shannon." She grabbed Sissy's hand and pulled her into the room. "Come on. You can braid my hair."

Sissy turned back to Jessie with a surprised look … and a hint of a smile.

Thank you, Jesus. Jessie breathed a silent prayer. *Tear down the barriers that are keeping Sissy from getting help. Direct us today so we can meet her needs.*

At Vera's nod, Jessie left the room to return to the crowd. She still hadn't talked with Nevin. Corbin hadn't lasted long in the kitchen, as he was already back talking to those who came in to eat, including her favorite veteran.

He looked from Nevin then back to her. "I'd describe Jessie as taking a bite of cranberry sauce. Little bit sweet with a tart kick at the end."

Jessie stopped and narrowed her eyes. She wasn't sure how to take Corbin's joke until his arm came around her again, like in the kitchen, and pulled her to his side. "But that's just one of the things I find so attractive about her."

Jessie's heart stilled. Had he actually admitted that … in front of everyone?

Chapter Sixteen

Jessie watched Corbin as he made his way around the room visiting those who had finished eating. People usually left soon after their meal, but not today. She was sure her husband was a main contributor to the fact. Sweet contentment wrapped around her heart in a pleasant sigh.

Familiar faces filled the room along with several new ones. Jessie searched for the woman with the baby she'd held last week. The mother hadn't come in. Although they couldn't help everyone, Jessie always hoped for the best with each case.

After gathering dishes and wiping down another table, she turned at the sound of Sissy's soft voice and saw her talking to Nevin.

"How come you're always in such a good mood?"

"The Bible says a lot about praising. I figure I should too." The elderly man looked across the room at the gray-blue sky. "We've all been given a cup to bear. And since I don't want folks remembering me for my complaints, I choose not to focus on the stuff floating around in my cup, but rather the One who gave it to me … and keeps it filled."

Sissy fidgeted with a loose button on her coat. "But doesn't it bother you, being next to homeless? Aren't you scared?"

"Scared? No. After you've had it all then lost it all, there's not much left to be afraid of." He glanced at the floor then back to Sissy. "Unless … you haven't come to terms with your immortality."

Sissy batted her eyes and looked away. "You can't be sure about any of that either."

In his kind, attentive way, Nevin coaxed her to divulge more. While keeping his focus on the windows, he asked, "What makes you say that?"

"I know you're going to tell me about God." Her nostrils flared as she fought an obvious urge to cry.

Jessie didn't know whether to move to the girl's other side in a show of support or stay put so as not to distract what Nevin might accomplish. She chose to continue cleaning the table.

Tears tracked down Sissy's cheeks as she stood with her arms wrapped around her, stiff as a wooden soldier. "I tried talking to Him. But it's hard to believe He's there when He won't stop the bad things." Her throat moved as she swallowed then wiped her cheek against her shoulder.

"I know. It is hard." Nevin's shoulders heaved with a heavy sigh. "But then I look around and see someone who's had it rough too and came through it all."

The emotions Sissy battled threatened to escape in their fullness. She hiccupped and asked, "Where do you see them?"

"Look around, girlie. They're right here, serving you with open hearts." Nevin turned and caught Jessie's hand. He pulled her over. "Like this one."

The man's face crinkled in a soft expression of admiration as he looked at Jessie. "This gal didn't let her experiences harden her heart. She kept it soft to help others out." He touched Sissy's shoulder. "Like you and me."

Jessie hugged Nevin's side. The smell of dirt and perspiration from his woolen jacket tickled her nose, but she held off the sneeze. She loved him and wouldn't let uncleanliness stop her from showing affection. Though she didn't know for sure, the shelter was probably the only place he received positive feedback.

Sissy stared at her with curious eyes. What was she thinking? Did she still not trust the workers' hearts at the shelter?

"Sissy?"

Jessie turned at the sound of Heather's voice. Heather ran over to the teen and swallowed her in a big hug. Although Sissy's response was a little rigid, she seemed to appreciate Heather's attention.

Heather pulled away and explained to Jessie. "This is my friend who would sometimes help me with the kids." She looked back at Sissy. "But I haven't seen her in a while."

Heather studied the teenager with questioning eyes. "I'm glad you're here. Come on, the boys will want to say hi." Heather didn't forget Jessie, but as she addressed her, the ease Heather had with the younger girl was replaced with the guarded personality Jessie knew. "I'll get the kids something to eat."

"Sure." Jessie understood. The sense of shame and failure were common with the homeless, as was rejection. She remembered being in their shoes and feeling no matter how much she wanted to trust, she couldn't shake the fear of being taken advantage of.

God, build their trust with those of us who want to help.

Aside from her works as proof, all that was left to do was pray.

***

Jessie's legs ached after leaving the shelter. She bent over in the front seat to rub them as Corbin turned into the local Dollar store. "What are you doing? Are we out of something?"

"I thought we could use a movie."

She watched him slip from the van as a silly grin lifted her cheek. What a perfect idea. Her eyes trailed Corbin as he strolled to the video box situated outside the store. No matter what the man threw on, he looked good. He stood with his weight to one hip and rested his arm on the machine as if he had all the time in the world. Well, from where she was sitting, he could take it. Jessie didn't mind at all.

"What's Dad doing?"

"Can we go home yet?"

Protestors from the back seat argued Jessie's unspoken opinion. The children had behaved better than she could've expected, but now were tired. She turned their attention away from their complaints.

"I'm really proud of how all of you helped out today."

"Did you see Layla playing with the little black-headed girl?" Shannon smiled proudly at her sister. "She was crying when the mom dropped her off, but Layla got her to stop."

"Yep. We played like we was wild an'mals."

Timmy spoke through a yawn. "I didn't like the guy with the black jacket."

Jessie couldn't remember seeing a young boy by that description, and she'd stopped by the game room several times. "When did he come in there?"

"He didn't."

"He'd just walk by the door and stare at us." Garrett finished for Timmy.

"How big was he?" Jessie held her breath and waited for an answer. Like anywhere, the shelter always held a mix of people. Some good. Some bad. She hoped they didn't mean the man she'd seen enter in a leather jacket covered in zippers. The look in his eyes had given her chills.

"He wasn't a boy, Mom," Shannon clarified. "More like Keith's age, but not nice like Keith."

Keith was a twenty's something at church. Jessie had known him for years and thought well of the young man, but this other one put her on red alert. As if they needed the reminder, they always kept two to three adults with the children. Jessie would talk to Vera and make sure at least one of those three would be a man from now on.

Corbin returned and dropped a movie in Jessie's lap. She recognized the title.

"Isn't this a romance?"

He darted his eyes as if uncomfortable she'd spoken the genre out loud. "*Comedy* romance."

Jessie bit her lip as her heart did a soft patter.

"Looky, it's 'towing!" Layla pointed as big snowflakes dropped against the van's window.

The boys began to plot the forts they'd build while Layla broke out in song from a recent Disney film.

"Do you wanna build a 'towman? It doesn't haf'ta be a 'towman..."

Corbin smiled beside Jessie and sighed with pleasure. "A perfect day."

At home, Jessie popped corn while Corbin unfolded the couch. He'd explained he and the kids would often watch a movie on the fold out bed, sometimes falling asleep there together.

Another blessing to count. Their families fit together better than she could've dreamed. Jessie hoped their bubble didn't pop.

She returned to the living room with the popcorn only to find Shannon hogging her dad's side. Disappointment threatened to steal Jessie's joy. But with four children in the room, she'd been silly to hope for a romantic evening.

"Time's up." Corbin patted Shannon's leg. "Let your momma sit there."

An instant pleasure filled Jessie's heart, but she didn't want to douse it with resentment from Shannon. "Will you sit by my other side? I'll share the big popcorn bowl."

A warm smile spread across her face. "Sure."

They snuggled up together on the bed with Layla at their feet and the boys on the floor with their toys between them.

Shannon reached for another handful of popcorn as the previews played. "I like you being here. Sometimes I wake up and still think it's just Garret, Dad, and me. Then I'll smell something good cooking and remember, oh yeah, I have a mom!"

Jessie hugged her and swallowed hard. The girl couldn't have said anything nicer. *Thank you, God. Thank you for allowing me to babysit them for the last couple of years.* She was sure that was the reason they'd adjusted so easily.

Fifteen minutes into the movie, the boys lost interest and focused on their play. Corbin turned up the volume to hear over their crashing car sounds and mimicking police sirens. "A little quieter guys."

With her belly full of popcorn and the comfort of the foldout bed, Jessie fought to keep her eyes opened. If Corbin had pulled her against his shoulder, she'd have conked out.

Layla plopped a baby doll in Corbin's lap. "She needs her daddy while I get her brother from school."

Corbin held the doll in his arms as if it were real. "Okay, I'll hold her as I watch the movie with your mommy."

Jessie laughed more at him than the film. He kept trying to remind the children he wanted to enjoy the movie with her, but they weren't getting the hint.

A long sigh streamed from his lips. Jessie leaned her head back against his arm draped across the cushion behind her. "It's the thought that counts, right?"

"Yeah." His eyes roamed over her face before he spoke again. "I'm proud of you and the work you're doing at the shelter."

"Really?"

"Everyone seems to know you there. And I think several were jealous when they learned we'd gotten married."

"You told them?" Though she didn't understand why, she was surprised he'd bring that up to others.

"Of course. I didn't like the way a lot of them were staring at you."

She poked his ribs in fun. "I thought it was great the way you kept conversation going with so many. That makes them feel important ... and worth something."

Corbin looked away as though considering those he'd met. "They're going through heavy stuff. A few have brought it on themselves, but like, Dale and Heather, some didn't have any control over their situations."

Jessie could see the day had taken its toll. No wonder he wanted a movie. He needed a distraction from the worry and sorrow. She turned back to the film and snuggled closer. To her surprise, his arm wrapped around her, securing her in place.

***

"I forgot!" Jessie shot up in bed.

Corbin blinked rapidly then rubbed a hand over his face. Shannon sighed from the edge of the rollout while Layla stirred at their feet.

"What are you talking about?" Corbin yawned and stretched.

"My mom's birthday's today. We always have it at our house."

"Okay," he shrugged.

"No, you don't understand. All her siblings come out, too."

"Huh?"

Jessie climbed over Shannon and picked up toy cars off the floor around the sleeping boys. "They didn't live around here when I was young. But now that they've all moved back, at least within driving distance, they always celebrate together."

"How many are we talking about?"

"Six."

Corbin's eyebrows rose.

"Plus spouses, and maybe a cousin or two. Well … and there was that one year Aunt June brought her neighbors."

***

A cold rain fell outside making it impossible for Corbin to escape the house. He inched his way through the throng of visitors toward the garage. After yesterday's fullness, he'd hoped for relative quiet today. Not *relatives*.

"Hey, nephew." Jessie's Uncle Ben pointed a finger at Corbin. "I can call you that now you and Jessie are hitched."

He'd made it as far as the stove. The garage door was only a yard away. He'd been so close. Corbin took a deep breath. "Yes."

"Since you're in town each week and I don't live too close, do you think you could pick my boots up from the store when they're done?"

"Your boots?"

"Yeah, I dropped them off today as we were going by. They needed resewn. Just pass them off to Samantha. She'll give them to Ruth when they get together and Ruth can bring them to me."

And why Uncle Ben didn't drive back in to get them was beyond Corbin. "Okay, no problem."

Ben fished in his shirt pocket and withdrew a small slip of paper, no bigger than a carnival ticket. "Here's the receipt. They'll have to be paid for when you pick them up. Can you cover seventy-four dollars until I see you again?"

Corbin's throat tightened and a pain zinged in his temple. "Why didn't you pay for them today?"

The man looked affronted that he would ask. "I didn't have it with me. Besides, why would I want to pay for a job that isn't done?" He pointed his finger again. "That's why you're the type that gets taken advantage of and I'm not."

Clearly, that's exactly what's happening now.

Laughter rose from the table as Samantha opened birthday cards, her course cackle loud enough to draw the attention of their neighbors. "That's a good card, but somebody forgot to sign it."

"No, I didn't." One of Jessie's aunt's spoke up. "I left it blank so you could reuse it."

Corbin shook his head. Already, one of them had given a card that someone else had given them before. The names had been marked through and the card resigned. He had no idea Jessie's family was so creative.

"What kind of engine is that on the hoist out there?"

Another of Jessie's uncles, pushed his way to the garage. For a brief moment, Corbin wondered how the man knew he had an engine at all. But, of course, the party had probably already been through the whole house.

Corbin followed the man to the garage. "It's a 369. Maybe one day I'll have the GTO it goes with, too."

"I know someone who has one."

Corbin wasn't serious about buying one now, yet he still liked talking shop. "Oh, yeah, what year is it?"

"A '66."

His favorite year, yet he knew it wasn't the right season in life to pour his time into a car. Still, for the sake of conversation and curiosity, he asked, "Who has it?"

The doorway darkened as Larry answered, "Max. Jessie's dad."

Jessie stepped into the garage. Her eyes narrowed at Corbin with a look of confusion and … hurt.

Chapter Seventeen

Jessie stumbled back from the door, her mind in a fog. Corbin couldn't contact her dad. He had no right.

Her mother's hoarse voice replied to something her aunt had said. Jessie watched them interact. Aunt June's face was soft where her mother's was marred with heavy lines. Years of smoking aged her. So had Max's decision when he'd left her in poverty to raise their child alone. He'd never so much as sent a birthday card or called to check on them … on Jessie.

The protective bubble of Jessie's youth returned. Memories of watching for him tore at her heart. She'd search the features of every dark haired man, hoping Max would come to rescue them. He'd never appeared.

Tears thickened her throat. Deep inside Jessie never stopped longing for a father. For Max—to apologize and explain. Had he been falsely accused and sent to prison or lost in the desert? Any story that meant he hadn't *chosen* to leave.

But life wasn't a fantasy.

For Corbin to contact him would be cruel. If Max came back into her life, he wouldn't stay. He'd only carve a greater chasm.

Someone gripped her elbow and pulled her past the table. Jessie fought her way back to the present. "Corbin?"

"We're going somewhere we can talk."

They stopped inside their bedroom and he closed the door.

Jessie wanted to speak first, to ask the questions tormenting her mind, but her tongue wouldn't move. Anger replaced weakness. Another protective emotion from her past. She brought her fist up, intent on pounding his chest.

Corbin caught her wrist. "I'm *not* contacting him."

Tears wet her lashes, making her angrier. "Then why did you ask about him?"

"I didn't."

Jessie stilled and struggled to regain control. "Explain, please."

"I was only making small talk with your uncle. He brought up cars, then your dad." Corbin released her. "You have a large enough family. Believe me, I see no need in adding to them."

A laugh of relief tumbled from her throat. He certainly had a point. She dropped her arm to her side. "So … you aren't even tempted?" Her heart froze with hope.

"Not at all."

"Not even for a car?" Her confidence shaken, she had to be sure.

"I have a dad," Corbin's features softened, "who's now yours too. Let's stick to that."

***

The next morning, Corbin sat at the table staring at the calendar now marred with a brown ring from his coffee mug. He swiped at it, smearing the stain then released a long sigh. The weatherman predicted snow and ice this week. If the ground hardened too much, the trees would take twice as long to pull which meant his crew wouldn't finish the jobsite on schedule.

Corbin rested his jaw in one hand. With the next job already secure, he shouldn't worry about starting late. Years of dedication built a trusted name for his business. He didn't want to lose that respect.

Jessie refilled his cup. "Want to share your troubles?"

He took a sip of the steaming liquid and appreciated how well Jessie saw to his needs. How did he overlook the fact for so long? "Aw, I'm just stressing over something I can't control."

"Like what?" She replaced the pot on the burner and turned to face him.

"Today's the best day to pull those trees for the extended parking lot, but it's Saturday and part of Thanksgiving vacation. I can't expect the guys to do it. If the weather forecast is right, this week won't help matters."

"Here," Jessie ran a cloth under the faucet.

Corbin studied the calendar again. If he went out today, he could manage to pull some of the trees himself, but without help, he wouldn't get very far.

Jessie came toward him but Corbin gave her actions little thought as he struggled with his decision. Her hand raised to his neck. Next, a sudden shock of icy cold paralyzed his skin.

Corbin jumped from his chair. The cloth toppled from his neck down the back of his shirt like a melting snowball.

"Ahh, ah," Corbin hopped to the side and pulled at the tail of his shirt. A drop of the chilled water trickled past his belt. Jessie started to help but doubled over, shaking and holding her sides.

Finally, the rag fell to the floor in a resentful heap. "What in the world, Jess?" He failed to share her humor.

Jessie snorted and fought to catch her breath. "I'm sorry. I read somewhere," she laughed and snorted again before she could explain, "a cold rag on your neck helps with stress. It has something to do with," she took another deep breath, "your hippo camper."

"Hippocampus," Corbin corrected as he stuffed his shirt-tail back in. "I read the same article at the hospital." He picked up the offending cloth and took it to the sink. The feel of the cold rag sent another shudder down his spine. "Trust me when I say … they were wrong."

"Maybe it only works in the summer time."

Yet another of Jessie's misguided decisions. At least she wasn't destroying the vinyl siding this time, or wreaking havoc with a ladder. "You can let me know by trying it on someone else."

Mischief and humor waltzed in her eyes. Corbin loved to see her lively and full of spirit, even at his own expense. He moved closer. She didn't back away, nor did her eyes lose their light.

"You owe me for that little bit of malpractice." He spoke in a low tone, not wanting to arouse any distraction from their children.

Jessie surprised him by inching closer and flirtingly walking her fingers up his chest. "Then send me the bill." She smiled wickedly before tossing her hair and spinning around.

Corbin caught her arm and pulled her back. Jessie's giggle smoothed into a sigh as his arms tightened around her. He bent his head toward her uplifted mouth. Blood pumped through his veins in a vigorous beat. Scents of amber and wildflowers teased his senses as his eager lips neared hers.

"B-ringgg. B-rinnggg."

Footsteps shuffled into the room. "Oh, gross." Shannon grabbed the receiver off the wall.

With reluctance, Corbin moved back. Jessie's look of longing drew a sigh of pleasure from his chest.

"It's for you, Dad." Shannon held a hand over her eyes as she offered the phone.

Corbin traced a finger over his wife's rosy hued cheek and whispered, "I'm not done with that down payment."

He put the phone to his ear while watching Jessie's color darken. He chuckled before speaking, "Hello."

"Corbin, you're always in such a good mood when we talk."

He frowned. "Who is this?"

"Oh, you silly bear, like you don't recognize my voice." A slight pause followed when he didn't answer. "It's Alyssa."

"Oh—hi." Why would she think he'd recognize her? They'd never spoken on the phone. "Do you want to talk to Jessie?" By this time, Jessie's attention was riveted on the phone. She glanced toward Shannon who still hadn't left. Shannon mouthed, "It's a woman."

Irritation balled in Corbin's throat. He didn't want to lose the mood they'd created. His hand tightened around the offending phone. "What can I help you with?"

***

Jessie drummed her fingers on top of the table. Standing here was ridiculous. She had dishes to put away and clothes to fold. One glance at Corbin affirmed she didn't want to stay in the room—not while he was talking to … a woman. That was enough to bristle her skin.

She moved toward the hall.

Corbin called out, "Don't go in the bedroom."

She looked back to see him uncover the phone and readdress the person on the other end of the line. What would it matter if she did? He could talk to her about the phone call when he was done. There was no reason to stay.

"Sorry I can't help. I have to go." Corbin hung up the phone and hurried past Jessie and blocked their bedroom door. "You can't go in there yet."

"Who was on the phone—I mean, why not?" She goofed, giving away her jealousy.

"Alyssa needed something fixed. I'm not a handyman, so I told her who to call."

Jessie felt her brows rise to her hairline. "*Alyssa.* I didn't know she had your number."

"Don't come in, until I put something away."

"What? It's just laundry."

"No. I forgot I set something out while going through the closet this morning."

Jessie frowned.

"It's a gift."

"For who, Alyssa longlegs?" Why couldn't she work a little harder to hide her emotions? Jessie moaned inside as a visible satisfaction lifted Corbin's chin.

"No. More like for Jessie just-right legs." His eyes dropped and slowly trailed up her length. "In fact, I think you should open the box today."

Stuck on the fact Corbin bought her a gift, Jessie wasn't sure how to respond. But considering what had been building in the kitchen and the way he now googled her, the gift was probably a sexy nightie—which meant he really bought himself a gift.

"I don't think so. No thanks."

"Don't you want to help me pull trees?"

Confused, Jessie looked up. "You want *me* to help you?"

"Sure. It's Saturday, and I'm sure your mom would watch the kids."

Jessie narrowed her eyes, contemplating the man blocking her path. What was he up to? "You obviously don't know my mom. She doesn't usually visit, yesterday was a rarity."

Corbin only shrugged before opening the door. "Sit down." He pointed to the bed.

Jessie did as commanded as he retrieved a box off the floor by the closet. He must have set it out after she had left the room.

"Sorry it's not wrapped, but here's an early merry Christmas."

The box was as big as the one her daughter's large unicorn arrived in last year. Surely Corbin hadn't bought her a stuffed animal. Jessie took a deep breath and opened the flap.

"Boots." She traced a finger over the oiled leather before lifting one from the box. Though they didn't sport a fancy heel like her pair from Tara, their design would still be suitable for church as well as everyday wear. "They're perfect. Thank you."

"That's not all."

She looked back in the box and removed the other shoe. Her heart leapt at what she hoped she saw through the thin layer of tissue paper. She greedily tore it away and grabbed at the red and black wool fabric.

Jessie's jaw dropped open when the folds fell from the coat. She stood and the box tumbled from her lap. "I can't believe it. You got me a coat like yours!"

"Well, it's not just like it, but as close as I could find."

"I have to try it on." She removed her sling then carefully slipped her arms through and twirled for him to see. "Do you like it?"

Corbin's eyes darkened and nearly glowed. "I love it."

The moment seemed to freeze in time as Jessie's heart fought to beat out of her chest. Judging from the look in Corbin's eyes and the husky quality of his voice, could he have been insinuating something else? Was he finally willing to fall in love?

With both hands, he lifted her hair from beneath the coat. The intimate action drew them closer. No longer did Jessie want to fight her feelings. Keeping her distance from this man had become too much of a challenge. She traced the top buttons of his shirt.

As though he couldn't contain his passion any longer, Corbin smashed her against him and pressed his lips against hers. Caught between them, pain shot through Jessie's sprained wrist. She gasped and wished she hadn't.

Corbin pulled away, his face lined with compassion and regret. "Oh, I'm sorry, Jessie. I forgot …"

"That's okay." She wanted to forget her wrist and refocus on their kiss, but pain thrummed its way up her arm.

"Maybe you shouldn't go out there with me today."

"No! I want to go. I'll put my sling back on and use my other arm."

"Go where? Can we come?" Both boys stood in the doorway with Layla squeezing her way between them.

***

Corbin helped lace up Jessie's boots. Although she'd been right and Samantha couldn't come over, Vera had readily agreed to keep them at her house.

He stood and watched Jessie test the new shoes. "How do they fit?"

"Great. And more insulated than my other ones."

Her smile wrapped around his heart, completing him. The recurring warmth he experienced all morning was back. His mouth pulled at the corner. It would be so easy to drop the kids off and come back with Jessie to an empty house.

Jessie's face winced in pain as Layla bumped into her wrist.

Oh, that doggone injury. Lord, help it heal ... and fast.

Corbin cleared his throat, hoping to help clear the heated desires continuously tempting him. "Let's get started." He clapped his hands together and strode to the door to retrieve his boots. They weren't there. Maybe he'd left them in the garage. He opened the door and looked. Again, he came up empty.

"Uh, oh. Are you looking for your shoes? They were kinda smelly so I thought I'd sit them outside while company was here yesterday." She grimaced, "but I forgot to bring them in." Jessie opened the front door. "Oh look, it's snowing!" The excitement in her voice rivaled that of the kids as they rushed to the door in awe.

Corbin squeezed past them and saw his work-boots on the porch, covered in a thick layer of frost ... and snow. He gritted his teeth to hold back a lecture on responsibility.

Chapter Eighteen

Jessie wiggled her toes inside her warm boots. "I really like my gifts. Thank you." Corbin's thoughtfulness overwhelmed her. She'd only begun to look online for gift ideas. When had he taken the time to shop?

"You're welcome." Despite how cold his feet must be, he smiled without guile. His lips twitched before his eyes dropped to her wrist. "I thought you'd be on the mend, but your arm seems to be giving you more trouble today."

"I tried to wash my hair this morning ... I think I reinjured it."

A crease formed over Corbin's brows and his jaw tightened. Why would he be angry? She relieved him the burden of washing her hair.

"Wish you hadn't." The comment was spoken as if to himself. "Was I not doing a good job?"

"No, I mean yes, you were. I just thought ... I don't want to add to your stress."

He looked from the road to her hair and his frown deepened. "Did you come out in this weather with it still wet?"

Jessie stiffened. *Here we go again.* She'd injured his pride by going around him and doing

198

something on her own. Jessie gave an indignant raise to her chin and smoothed the crown of her head. "I'm smart enough to know to blow dry my hair—" Her hand paused at the back of her hair.

Corbin's lip curled. "It's dirty, isn't it?"

"It's not dirty." Jessie slapped his arm. "I must've missed getting all the shampoo rinsed out."

"Which means it's dirty."

Jessie rolled her eyes and turned toward the window. The man could be so exasperating.

Stopped at a traffic light, Corbin turned her head to examine her find. She jolted at the touch of his hand. "I'll wash it out tonight. Until then," he opened the console and withdrew a ball cap, "you can wear this."

"Is it that bad?"

He shrugged. "I know you. And in case we run into anyone you know, you'll feel better this way."

She plopped the cap down tight and slumped in the seat. How did he know her so well in such a short amount of time? Had he paid that much attention all those years she'd watched his children?

***

From the seat of a bulldozer, Jessie listened while Corbin explained the levers he wanted her to use. She could picture him using his authoritative voice to command people on the site each day. He was a good leader. The nearly completed plaza, and the crew with very little turnover, was proof of that.

His nearness brought with him the comforting scent of his cologne. Jessie inhaled and let her gaze trail his short cut hair to his wool coat blanketing strong, sturdy shoulders. With her eyes closed, she saw him climbing into bed, his stomach and arm muscles lithe. Her lips curved in a slow smile before lazily lifting her lids.

Corbin stopped talking and watched her with a curious expression. "Should we have stayed home?" The smoothness of his voice matched the aroma of his cologne.

"Ahem." Jessie felt her cheeks burn. "I was just … listening."

When he didn't move, she grabbed a lever. "This one goes forward to make the bucket go up, right?"

Corbin scrunched his mouth to the side then shook his head. "The other way, Jess."

"Oh, yeah. I got it, don't worry."

After another long, smoldering look, he slid off the step and went to work wrapping a chain around one of the trees. Although none of them were very big, as he'd explained to her earlier, their root systems might give them trouble.

Jessie squirmed in the cold seat and tried to get comfortable. He'd been serious. He would've left the trees alone and eagerly taken her home. Why had she brushed him off like that? *God, I don't know why I'm having trouble accepting his hints. Please help me out. I don't want to keep pushing him away.*

"Take her up." Corbin gave her a thumbs up.

"Okay," Jessie spoke to herself as she gripped the lever, "it goes the opposite of what I think it should. That means … back."

Relief washed over her with the climb of the bucket. The chain links clunked as they tightened against the pull of the dozer. Jessie peeked around the side to see a root fling from the earth in a spray of snow and dirt. The tree shook as the chain slipped up the trunk, finding a hold beneath a slender branch. Within moments, the tree was free.

"Okay, that's good."

Jessie turned, her concentration broken by another sound. Corbin stood with his hands cupped over his mouth. "You can stop!"

"Oh, okay." She released the lever, proud of her accomplishment. "We make a good team, huh?"

Corbin chuckled. "Yeah, just bring the bucket back down so I can reach it."

Jessie pulled back then remembered to push forward. The bucket rattled with her indecision before lowering.

Corbin unhooked the chain, tossed it over the bucket then climbed the step beside her. "Now you can learn to drive."

"No, I don't think I'm ready for that." She glanced at the levers where there should have been a steering wheel.

"Okay, then watch as I move us a few feet over."

Corbin slid his arm behind the seat and brought his foot within inches of hers to operate the pedal. A few maneuvers later, he'd changed their position. "Easy."

"Nothing about your job is easy," Jessie admired her contractor husband, "but I enjoy being out here with you."

A muscle in his jaw flexed as he scanned her face. His scrutiny falling from her eyes, to her nose then her lips before concentrating on the snowflakes accumulating in Jessie's hair. Finally, Corbin's warm expression rested for a brief moment on her arm in the sling. With a short sigh, he turned and hopped down.

Jessie waited for Corbin to secure another tree with building resentment toward her injury. Didn't the man know he could work around the sling? Though tickled by the brazen thought she kept a smile from erupting. Corbin needed the lot cleared. Which meant they had to stay focused.

***

The bucket whined as it rose to its highest point. Corbin waited patiently while his wife stared off to the side. Like before, once the bucket stopped with a jerk, she'd pull her mind back to the job.

He shook his head. Should he lecture Jessie again about paying attention or just laugh? At least she wasn't a paid employee.

The bucket shook as it came to a stop. He heard Jessie's surprised response. *Where is her mind this morning?* With a switch of the lever, the bucket lowered to where Corbin could reach the tree. "Okay, that's enough," he signaled.

After unhooking the chain and towel he used to pad the trunk, he looped another nearby tree and stepped to the side. He signaled and said, "Take her up."

Jessie nodded and leaned forward. With a loud thud, the bucket dropped to the ground. Corbin jumped back to save his toes from being smashed.

"Oh, sorry. I keep forgetting which way is up and which way is down. Are you sure these aren't backwards somehow?"

"Not for the rest of us, they aren't," he mumbled and rubbed his forehead then glanced at the remaining property. Half done. This was going to be a long, cold day.

After another hour, Corbin climbed the step beside Jessie's seat. "How about a lunch break?"

"Oh, good. I'm freezing."

Corbin noted her red nose and chattering teeth. "Why didn't you tell me you were so cold?" He helped her down and rubbed his hands over her upper arms.

Jessie leaned forward and buried her nose in his coat. "I didn't want to complain."

Despite her squirrel-like attention span today, Jessie was a hard worker. He proudly walked her to the truck. "We'll warm up with soup."

As they entered the restaurant line, overhead speakers greeted them with holiday music. Jessie hugged her arms to herself. "Oh, I love listening to Bing Crosby croon."

Corbin inclined his ear. The lyrics promised something about the more you gave the more you'd get. The verse repeated itself wrapped in a catchy tune. He glanced at his wife's attire. His giving had just begun. Next ... he planned to offer his heart.

Trepidation seized him. *She won't refuse, will she God?* Jessie had every right. He hadn't exactly started with the right attitude.

And what if she did? The idea of his love not being accepted ... or returned ... left his chest hollow. He absently rubbed a hand over his heart. Is this what she felt like? The idea struck him with force. Could Jessie already love him? Had he refused *her*?

Guilt squeezed him like a vice. He was far from the man she deserved. Scenes of the last two weeks sped through his memory. The only thing he'd offered was his body.

He dropped his head and sighed. What a scoundrel he'd been, completely oblivious to the gift God had given him. He couldn't waste any more time. He cupped Jessie's shoulder.

Jessie sneezed, the force of which drew her forward out his grasp, followed by two more.

"Next in line, please." The attendant called to take their order. Before Corbin could decide what to do, Jessie was at the counter listing the soup she preferred.

They found their seats in the middle of the busy lunch crowd. Corbin glanced at those eating within a couple feet of them. He'd have an audience for sure. He closed his eyes and drew a breath ...

"Why didn't you just push the trees over?"

"What?" Corbin stared across the table. He'd been ready to profess his love and Jessie wanted to talk about trees?

"Wouldn't that have been faster?"

"Probably." He stirred his soup. Steam swirled into the air. "But we were asked to save as many as possible and replant them intermittently around the grounds." Again, feeding his reputation. Word would get out about his company's environmental care. His mouth set into a grim line. Time to reconsider who he served—and put God at the top of the list.

Jessie sneezed again and shuddered. "Oh, I'm still so cold."

Her fall had been a big enough scare to Corbin. He didn't want her to get sick, too. "I think we've uprooted enough to replant. Let's enjoy our soup and call it a day."

He asked the blessing and added a silent plea for another opportunity.

When they were finished with their lunch, Corbin drove to Wade and Vera's to get the children. Jessie half dozed beside him, worn out from the wind and the cold. Her head bobbed forward and she straightened with a start. She cleared her throat and gave a sleepy eyed look toward Corbin. He sighed. She had no idea how irresistible she was.

"Oh," Jessie covered her yawn. "Don't know why I'm so tired."

"The weather will do that to you." He lifted the console to its upright position and patted the seat beside him. "Slide over here and rest against my shoulder."

Her chin jerked toward him. Jessie's eyebrows rose then her mouth softened into a pleased expression. She undid her seatbelt in exchange for the middle one and inched her way over. With a pleasant sigh, the weight of her head settled against him, and she fell back to sleep.

Corbin adjusted the mirror to glance at his dark-haired angel. Her hat had risen halfway off her head, comical, but it didn't detract from her beauty.

Thick black lashes contrasted against her wind burned cheeks. Her lips were extra bright. Probably chapped from the weather.

I have a beautiful wife.

The trumble slits vibrated the truck tires. The sharp, rip-rap directed Corbin's attention back to driving. He swung back into his lane and for their safety, readjusted the mirror. He'd found Jessie distracting before, but being married only amplified his feelings.

He glanced from the window to her glove-clad hands resting next to his thigh. Throwing caution to the wind, he held the steering wheel in his left hand and scooped hers up with the other. Where the glove and sleeve exposed her wrist, he placed a kiss. The first of what he hoped would be many, many more.

***

"What's up with the ball cap?" Wade tugged the bill of Jessie's cap over her eyes.

"It kept her warm today." Corbin inserted. "And since I let her get too cold, it's probably still keeping her warm." He hoped his explanation would save her embarrassment.

"Corbin's just protecting my dignity. Truth is, I thought I'd save him the trouble of washing my hair and hurt my wrist trying to do it myself ... and still didn't get it clean."

"Need me to wash it for you?" Vera offered.

"No thanks. Corbin likes holding my head under the sink faucet."

A chuckle rose from the adults as a warm tug pulled at Corbin's heart. Yes, he did. He enjoyed anything that brought him into contact with Jessie.

As they sat and visited, Corbin tuned into Jessie and Vera's conversation while Wade answered a call. The women discussed the young girl from the shelter.

"I understand where you're coming from." Vera's gentle eyes watched Jessie. "God has given you compassion toward broken hearts."

"It's frustrating watching people self-destruct. I'm afraid she's one of them." Jessie sighed. "I'd like to change her. Change her way of thinking, the way she lives, the way she doesn't take care of herself."

"Remember what Wade has said, "It's not our job to do something *to* them, but *for* them." Don't let your goal of wanting a better life for her overwhelm what she needs right now."

"I know, but she needs a permanent place to stay. People to trust—"

"What she needs, is to feel loved. You need to meet her where she's at, without expectation of change. Do you remember why?"

Jessie chewed her lip and thrummed her fingers along the table. With a sheepish sideways glance toward Corbin, she returned her attention to Vera. "Yes. It's like your husband said a couple of weeks ago. It's their world, their house. It's only right we must be invited in."

"And we only get invited in by showing them love." Vera smiled and rubbed the top of Jessie's hand. "God didn't lay this burden on your heart to let you stumble over yourself. So wipe the worry from your face. He'll guide you."

Corbin slid his arm across the back of Jessie's chair, brushing his fingers along her shoulders, and leaned toward her. "We'll pray about it together and see where God's leading that soft heart of yours."

***

Light filtered through the bedroom window as Corbin squinted, not willing to open his eyes. They'd shopped for groceries after leaving the pastor's house. Once home and the food put away, Jessie's hair washed and the children put to bed, Corbin was more than happy to call it day. He'd slept heavy, never waking.

He rotated his wrist, sending tingles of sleep through his arm. A weight prevented him from moving. He peeked through slatted lids. Pleasure encompassed his heart. Jessie nestled in his arms. It was the first time they cuddled this close. He snuggled nearer and released a contented sigh. This was what a marriage should be like.

Jessie bolted straight up, her arm smacking Corbin's face. "Nine o'clock!"

"What?" He rubbed his bruised eye.

"We overslept." Jessie scrambled to her feet, towing tangled covers halfway off the bed.

Corbin looked in amazement at his bedside clock. She was right. How would they ever get everyone ready in time for Sunday school?

The morning passed in a flurry of commotion with children bumping into each other and quarreling over the smallest things. By the time they made it to church, Corbin craved coffee. He yawned while Jessie signed Layla into her class.

They fell into step with one another. Slightly irritated, he asked, "Why are you always hugging everybody?"

"I don't hug everyone." Jessie quickened her pace, leaving him to trail behind.

He'd lit her spitfire. The havoc morning had caught up with everyone.

"You just hugged Layla's teacher. You hugged that other woman in the hall. You hugged your friend yesterday at the restaurant."

Jessie came to an abrupt halt. Corbin teetered forward and caught his balance before toppling on top of her. He scowled once he realized she'd stopped to talk to a young man. A man who never once acknowledged Corbin. Maybe he wasn't here the Sunday they married. Corbin couldn't expect everyone to know, yet the fingers of jealousy still tightened around his heart.

He considered holding Jessie's hand—in a way that would show off the ring he'd placed on her finger, but the short conversation ended.

Jessie smiled, "Nice to see you, Keith."

The guy reached over for a hug before parting ways.

"Perfect," Corbin mumbled, "here we go again."

As they continued toward the sanctuary, Jessie shrugged. "I didn't realize I was such a huggy person. So big deal. I like to hug."

"You've never hugged me."

Jessie stopped. Corbin caught himself again to keep from falling on his wife. Was she trying to break his neck? Others brushed by them in the hallway.

Somewhere it seemed a persistent drum kept a steady beat. Corbin couldn't blurt out, "I love you." Not when Jessie would think he was mocking her.

"I'm not the only guilty party." She shuffled her Bible and notebook in her arms. "You've never hugged me either."

He smirked, loving her spunk. "Then it's time I did." He moved toward her but Jessie backed against the wall.

"Not now. Not here." She hissed. "You'll only make a scene."

Chapter Nineteen

Jessie met Tara Monday morning as she opened the garage door. "Climb on in," she pointed to the passenger side of the van, "it's too cold to stand out here." The temperature had dropped again. Her warm breath formed puffs of vapor.

"Might be cold, but isn't the snow pretty?" Tara settled beside Jessie.

"Beautiful. And since the trees at the lot are pulled, maybe Corbin can enjoy it too." The thought popped out of her mouth, but if felt good to talk to someone about Corbin. For the past week, he'd monopolized her mind.

"Speaking of which," a dimple formed in Tara's cheek as she tucked the side of her mouth and raised an eyebrow, "how are things?"

"We're doing good."

"*Just* good?"

Jessie laughed to cover her embarrassment, but Tara's questioning was her own fault. She'd told her of their odd marriage. "Things are going in the right direction. And honestly, if it weren't for my wrist, we'd probably be normal by now."

"How long does a sprain take to heal?"

"It's not *just* that. There's four kids that keep us hopping, the shelter … the phone."

"Wait." Tara's hand shot up and covered the center of the steering wheel. Jessie stopped at the end of her drive. "You hesitated. What about the phone?"

A long sigh preceded her answer. "Alyssa called Saturday."

Tara responded with another hooked brow.

"But enough about my mess. How's yours? Did last week fix a few things?"

Tara narrowed her eyes suspiciously before answering. "It was a good patch. One day I'll tell you more about it, but not until you and Corbin are in a good place. 'Cause believe me, two negatives don't make anything right!" Tara pressed for more information, "So what did your nemesis want?"

Jessie smirked. Tara was a true friend. "Supposedly, she needed Corbin to fix something." She held up a hand to stop Tara from going off on a tangent. "Corbin gave her the number of someone who does handyman work and got off the phone."

"Err, that girl! And she's so obvious. It's not like she even tries to hide her attraction to him." Tara's frown turned into a slow, purposeful smile. "Are you going to the Christmas party at the pastor's house this week?"

"Of course." Jessie never missed. Wade and Vera's holiday get-together was one of the many highlights of the season.

"I'll bring some kale chips and offer them to Corbin."

"What will that do?"

"Solve your problems." Tara chuckled like a kid pulling a prank.

The thought of food made Jessie's stomach growl. She and Tara hadn't had lunch together in almost a month. She looked forward to their meal.

The sun glinted off a metal piece of trash on the side of the road. Jessie averted her eyes from the bright light just in time to see a ball of fur bound into the road.

"No!" Jessie swerved to avoid hitting the animal. Her tire bumped against the concrete curb separating the road from the resident's lawn. With a quick turn of the wheel, she righted the vehicle back in her lane.

"Crazy cat!" Her hands shook as she realized how close she'd come to wiping out someone's mailbox, along with the front end of the van.

"Why can't your neighbor show a little respect for the rest of the neighborhood?" Tara knew all about Mrs. Clarkson and her troublesome habits.

"Don't worry. We have a plan to fix the problem." As Jessie drove into town, she explained Corbin's idea that would also help Heather and Dale. Though she'd hoped Dale could've started on the project already, he promised to soon.

Two blocks from the coffee shop, the van became hard to steer and a repeating *thwarp*, *thwarp* sounded against the pavement. "Something's wrong. The car's pulling really hard."

Tara rolled down the passenger window and stuck her red head out, unconcerned for the damage the wind was doing to her style. "You've got a flat. Pull over to the side."

Jessie sighed. She'd never been good at changing tires. It seemed the lug nuts were always tightened by Hercules. She slipped the transmission into park and turned off the engine. After getting out and meeting Tara beside the back tire, she asked, "I can only use one arm. Are you any good at this?"

"Hah, I work at a hair salon, not a tire shop." She glanced at her reflection in the back window and calmed her tousled waves. Tara walked to the back of the van and lifted the door. "But I'm sure we can figure it out together."

A truck slowed to a mere crawl and an elderly man rolled down his window. After hanging his arm over the side of the door and looking over their situation, he drawled, "Havin' car trouble?"

"Flat tire," Tara answered.

"Ye-ep." The man gave a slow nod and proceeded to drive away.

Jessie gawked. Was he really leaving?

Beside him, one of the female passengers turned and waved through the back window. Jessie squinted. "She looks familiar."

"Too-da-loo!" The British accent taunted Jessie.

"Oh, that woman! I want to … I want to …"

"Whatever you decide, I want to be in on it."

Jessie looked at Tara as a laugh tumbled from her throat. "I don't know what I'd do without you."

After several minutes of both of them alternating between jumping up and down on the four-way lug wrench, it was evident Jessie and Tara lacked the proper skills to change a tire.

Jessie let her back fall against the van. "I give up." She brushed hair from her face. "Maybe I'm not supposed to have a stress-free lunch without children or be able to order dessert without splitting it three ways."

Tara snorted. "Is that what this is about? God doesn't think you should have a moment to yourself?"

"Can you think of any other reason?"

As if God had chosen to answer for Himself, a familiar voice called to Jessie.

"You need help?" Sissy strode up beside them, clad in a thin hoodie, short skirt, and tights. She had to be freezing.

"Sissy, it's good to see you." Jessie motioned to the flat. "I'll have to call a tire shop."

Tara explained their unsuccessful efforts. "It wouldn't even budge with us jumping on it."

"Have you tried using a driver to hit it?"

"A what?" Jessie and Tara answered simultaneously.

"You know, like having a wrench on it then hitting the wrench with a hammer. It'll loosen the crud."

Jessie scratched her head. "I would've never thought of that, but it's worth trying. Only, I don't have a hammer."

Sissy turned around and foraged the side of the road and ditch. She came back holding a sizable rock. "Here, stand back." With the four-way still secured over the nut, she hammered it with the rock several times. "Okay, now we'll try."

Jessie watched in amazement as the young girl, much thinner than herself, wrenched the lug nut free. "Wow, you're amazing."

"Nah, just resourceful." She stepped back as if to leave.

"Don't go anywhere." With Tara holding the lug wrench, Jessie repeated Sissy's method with her good arm to loosen another bolt. "After we get this changed, we'll all go out to lunch."

Sissy's mouth parted in evident surprise. "You don't have to do that."

"I know, but I want to." She stood and let Tara take over. "If you'll give me a chance, I'd like to be your friend."

Sissy's head shot up, as if the idea was foreign. Her questioning gaze soon glazed over with a feigned look of interest. "Maybe." She shrugged, "Nevin seems to think you're okay."

"I should hope. He's a good friend of mine."

"Really?" The question was spoken in disbelief.

"I've made a lot of friends through the shelter. And I really meant what I said about us being friends. You can never have too many."

Tara moaned. "Okay, Sissy, since you're the smartest of us three, how about you explain how to get the spare out from under the van?"

A small guffaw sounded from the teen. She shook her head as if exasperated at their limited skills, but a smile broke through her charade.

Sissy found the tire iron beneath a pile of shopping totes and kid clothes. "See this hole," she pointed above the back door latch. "Slip this end of the iron in there and turn."

"Oh," Jessie folded over to see the tire secured beneath the van. She held onto her hair to keep it from dragging on the dirty snow. "I remember Richard showing me that once."

"Is he your husband?" Sissy continued to crank the wheel extending the tire and cable.

"Was." Jessie dragged the tire closer.

"Here, let me." Tara took her place. She lifted one end up to remove the cable from the wheel. "Oh, these things are heavy."

Back on the road, Jessie made a short detour to the tire shop before stopping for lunch. "You know, that flat probably happened when I swerved to miss the cat. I saw something on the side of the road and judging from the cut in the tire, I bet that's what caused it."

"Don't give it anymore thought or you'll just get heated again at your cat lady."

"Are you talking about the woman who feeds her cats in the road?" Sissy stepped through the door Jessie held open.

"Yes, how did you hear about her?"

"Heather told me."

"Oh yeah, she mentioned you're the friend who used to watch her kids to give her a break."

"Yeah, we'd take them to the park and stuff. They're really cute. Ornery ... but cute."

Their orders came and the table grew silent as they enjoyed the first few bites.

Sissy looked around. "I've never been in here." Her eyes took in the coffee décor. "It's relaxing. Smells good, too."

Had Sissy grown up in this town, or was it true, she moved around a lot? Until she gained her trust, Jessie couldn't expect her to open up. She looked from Sissy to Tara in search of safe conversation. "Did you know Tara's a beautician here in town? She's usually the only one I let touch my hair."

Sissy watched them both. "Usually?"

Jessie held up her sling. "My husband has to wash it since I goofed on the ice."

"Oh." Her brows raised, wrinkling her forehead. "Does he make a good *beautician*?"

Jessie enjoyed seeing the girl lighten up. "The manliest." Just the mention of her favorite subject and Jessie's thoughts stuck to Corbin. After running yesterday morning back through her mind, she was certain she'd awakened to his arm around her. The thought made her skin sizzle. Too bad she hadn't been awake when he got out of bed this morning. Would he hold her tonight? She hoped so.

"Where'd she go?"

"Day-dreaming. She just got married, you know."

"What?" Jessie refocused on Tara and Sissy. "What were you saying?"

"She said you just got married? How many times does this make?"

Jessie tried to cover her shock at the girl's question but couldn't keep her eyes from widening. "My second. My first husband died."

"Oh." Sissy was quiet a moment. "Sorry. I just figured you'd been married a lot like most of my mom's friends. My mom, though, has had a lot more boyfriends than husbands."

"Is that why you stay with friends?" Jessie almost wished she hadn't asked. *Almost.* In reality, she wanted to know as much as Sissy would tell.

What made a young girl think she could survive better on the streets than in her own home?

She cringed at the possible scenarios that entered her mind. Maybe she didn't really want to know.

"Partly." Sissy focused her attention on her food and finished her sandwich in silence. Jessie and Tara did the same.

The surrounding warmth and contentment of a full stomach seemed to relax Sissy. She propped an arm on the table. "I bet you two have been friends forever."

Jessie answered, "Quite a few years." She waited for the girl to share her thoughts.

"It's lonely ... being out there."

Compassion filled Jessie's heart, making her eyes sting. "Where do you stay?"

"I couch surf. You know, stay with friends here and there. But they're not good for me to be around, ya know?"

Jessie shook my head. She didn't know.

"'Cause of their habits. I don't want to be like them."

"Oh. I know our shelter is full at the moment, but have you checked with other shelters?"

"Nah, too many bed bugs." Her hand flew up. "Not that yours has 'em, I just mean, most of the ones I've been in do."

"I understand." Jessie's thoughts collided in a frenzy of solutions. Should she offer their home, call other shelters?

Vera's advice flooded Jessie's thoughts. *"If you really want to make a difference in her life, shower her with love. Every day, find some way to contact her and prove your sincerity."*

"How can I keep in touch with you?"

"I've been coming to the shelter more. There's some good cooks there." She smiled again, lighting up her face.

"That's good to know. We only serve what we like to eat."

Tara reached for her coat. "As much as I've enjoyed this, I have to go. Justin and I made a little agreement last week. He'll come home at a better time, and I'll put more effort in the house. So ... looks like I've got some catchup work to do and a dinner to fix."

Sissy followed them to the door. "I appreciate you taking me out."

"You're welcome." Jessie threw an arm over the girl's thin shoulders and squeezed. "And thank you for coming with us and helping change the tire. Can I give you a ride somewhere?"

"Naw, I like to walk." She shuffled her feet as if she had something else to say. "You know, most people won't look me in the eye, let alone take the time to listen. Thanks again. For treating me like I'm somebody."

Jessie batted her eyes to keep from crying. "Of course." *God sees you, too. He knows you're somebody.* The words stalled on the end of her tongue. Sissy's life hadn't been easy. It would take time before she'd be ready to receive encouragement about God. But Jessie planned to be there when she was. A game plan was already forming. One Corbin would support.

Chapter Twenty

Corbin listened as Jessie described her encounter with Sissy. Excitement illuminated her face, giving her an ethereal appearance. He fought to focus on her words.

"… and after we changed the tire, we all went out to lunch …"

Although he'd warned her against transporting people she didn't know, the fact Tara had been with her helped. When she finished, he asked, "So how do you plan to build a relationship with Sissy if you don't know where she lives?"

"She said she's coming to the shelter more. I want to stop by each day and whether or not she's there, leave something for her."

"Like what?"

"For starters, a warm coat. She's always wearing a thin hoodie. She has to be cold. But I also plan on leaving cards or letters. That way she won't just receive material things, but part of my heart."

Corbin's chest swelled. Jessie had a heart of gold. He moved to brush hair from her lashes, but she was too excited to notice. She turned and paced in front of him.

"I want to earn her trust so she'll see Jesus through me and eventually want to know Him, but I need to prepare for the questions she's going to ask. Like what she asked Nevin about why God allows bad things to happen." She stopped and met his gaze. "How do I explain that?"

"Have a seat." He guided his little ball of energy to the table, then said a silent prayer for wisdom as he considered how to answer. Her inquiry was one often asked by believers and nonbelievers alike. Corbin rubbed a hand over his face then chose to start with a question of his own. "What would the world be like if God didn't allow evil?"

"Perfect, like Heaven, I guess."

"And how could we, as mortals, live that way?" He waited a moment before giving her the answer. "We can't unless we no longer have the freedom to choose."

"Okay," Jessie rubbed her temple. "I'm going to try to think like Sissy and ask what she might ask. So based on what you're saying, couldn't God have just not created evil then it wouldn't matter about having the freedom to choose?"

"He didn't create evil. He simply created the potential for evil. You see, God wanted us to have the ability to experience love, but in order for that to happen He had to give us free will to choose whether or not we would love. And by doing that, He created the potential for evil because that was the only way to create the potential for genuine love."

"Hmm ... so the bad stuff happens because of our choices ... but I wish the innocent didn't have to suffer because of it."

"Who's innocent? Romans says we've all sinned and fallen short of the glory of God. We're all sinful by nature, even babies. God didn't create the world this way though, and one day He'll right it again. But until then, what the devil intends for bad, He uses to draw us to Him."

Jessie nodded in understanding. "Okay. That makes sense." Her brows relaxed. She sat back in her chair and stared at the wall for a few moments. Then she cocked her head to the side. Her eyes narrowed as if challenged by another deep thought. Slowly, she turned to study Corbin.

Now what was she thinking? Whatever it was, despite his biblical explanation, Corbin had a sinking feeling of guilt.

"Maybe you should try pondering that some things are a choice." Jessie rose from the table. Corbin couldn't leave his chair fast enough to stop her. He had to let her know—he didn't need to ponder anything. He'd already fallen head over heels in love.

The chair toppled backward. A loud whack sounded as oak hit the tiled floor.

"What was that?!" Kids came running into the kitchen. Next came the wails of hunger, followed by complaints about the choice of dinner, and the typical aggravation of siblings. Regardless of the chaos, Corbin took a deep breath to shout above the commotion when a knock rapped at the front door.

Really?

Corbin crossed the living room and opened the door to his new friend. "Dale, come on in."

"Oh, I can't, my family's in the car. I just stopped by to see when we can discuss the plans for your neighbor's yard. She has some fancy ideas, but I thought I'd run them by you … and find out who's paying for it."

"Who's paying for it?" Jessie overheard and stood with a hand on her hip, her mouth set for battle.

Corbin gritted his teeth. Between Mrs. Clarkson and Alyssa, his marriage could easily freeze over. *God, this house needs an Indian summer.*

***

The next evening, Corbin held the door open for his family to exit the school. A cold winter wind threatened to rip the door from his hold. He pulled his collar up to shield his neck.

Shannon's final play practice. *Thank goodness.* He was ready to slow down and have more evenings at home.

Yesterday, when Corbin wouldn't take no for an answer, Dale had agreed to stay to discuss work at Mrs. Clarkson's. Since Jessie overheard his announcement, Corbin had to assure her they wouldn't be paying the cost. Dale's family ate dinner with them, making for a late evening. Tomorrow they'd attend the annual Christmas party at the pastor's house. Thursday the play and then he hoped nothing was planned for the weekend.

"Did someone call me?" Shannon darted out of the family huddle as they hurried to the van.

"Shannon!" A girl waved to her from the front of the school.

"That's the one I told you about a couple of weeks ago." Jessie whispered to Corbin through chattering teeth.

Corbin narrowed his eyes as he watched over his daughter. "Are things better?"

"I haven't heard."

Shannon stopped beside the girl. A few words were spoken then Shannon gave her a hug.

When she returned, Corbin ushered them to the van and started the engine. Once heat poured through the vents, he flipped on the interior light and craned his head toward the back. "What was that about?"

In her shy, humble way, Shannon raised a shoulder toward her cheek. "She wanted to thank me."

"What for?"

She fiddled with a bracelet around her wrist. "Don't be mad …"

Never a good start to a sentence. Corbin braced himself for what he undoubtedly didn't want to hear.

"I gave her my Bible."

A band tightened around his throat. Her mother had chosen the Bible for her. If Shannon had only asked, he would've bought one for the girl.

Shannon offered, "She probably won't keep it. I just thought if she would read some of it, she might understand—"

Corbin cleared his throat. "It's okay if she does, honey." In the recent lessons he'd learned, he was here to serve God, not his business … or sentiments. "You're simply passing on the example set by your mom."

Her eyes misted. Corbin had no doubt his daughter had done the right thing. Perhaps owning a Bible with Shannon's name, and that of her deceased mother's, would prompt the girl to value it more than one new from the store.

He swallowed hard and straightened back in his chair. Slipping the transmission into drive, he pulled out of the parking lot. The kids settled into usual chatter while he and Jessie sat quietly up front.

Jessie's hand covered his, sending a rush of warmth up his arm. She squeezed slightly then started to pull away. Did he want her to? A tremor caught him off guard as her fingers slid across his skin. *No, don't let go.* How could this small gesture cause such a deep response?

Perhaps a little too eagerly, Corbin turned his hand to catch the ends of her fingers. Her round eyes said she was as surprised as he was. He searched for something to say. "Um ... thanks ... for your support," he whispered.

She rubbed her thumb across his finger. "I lo—" Jessie coughed and briefly glanced out the window. "You'll always have my support."

Had she almost said ...

Corbin's heart seemed to stall with his breath. If she loved him, why hadn't she said so? He'd gladly tell her the same. Doubt heckled him like a bully on the playground. She had every right to give up. He hadn't been a good husband. He wanted to change. He *was* changing. But was it already too late?

Like needles to his heart, sleet pinged against the windshield, blurring his vision. The tires slipped as ice built up on the road. Time to get both hands on the wheel.

***

Jessie stomped the snow off her boots on the rug inside the beauty salon.

Tara looked up from lathering color onto the strands of someone's hair. "Hey, I didn't expect to see you today."

"You got a minute?"

"Sure." Tara pointed to the woman in the chair. "She's about to go under the dryer."

Moments later, she left the noisy dryer and joined Jessie on the other side of the room. "I have an opening if you're ready to let me highlight that mane? I think a little fiery red would be just the thing."

"Ha. I'm too cheap for that. Which, ironically, is the reason I'm here. Remember offering me a brown coat that you said was too snug?"

"Sure. It's in that closet. I still haven't found anyone who needs it."

"Sissy does."

Tara gasped. "That's right! Why didn't I think of that?"

Jessie opened the closet door and removed the wool, knee length coat. "Was this your mom's?"

"No. An elderly client gave it to me."

"Hmm ... what if she sees Sissy wearing it." Jessie drew her bottom lip between her teeth. Maybe she should've gone to the thrift store instead. "She might be offended you gave it away."

"Not at all. The Lord's already called her home. Besides, I think she'd be thrilled the coat will serve such a need. She was a wonderful Christian woman, a prayer warrior. In fact, I think my marriage is suffering from her absence."

Jessie studied her friend. What wasn't she telling? "Did Justin enjoy his home cooked meal last night?"

"I guess. You know we communicate like a train whistle to a car on the tracks, so who knows." Tara cleaned her tools and looked at Jessie through the mirror. "So how are you and Corbin?"

"Uh … I almost talked too much last night." Jessie sighed. "I nearly said I loved him … *out loud.*"

Tara frowned. "And why didn't you?"

"Because … he already told me he doesn't want to love me."

A low whistle sounded from Tara's lips. "And I thought Justin and I had troubles."

***

Jessie glanced in the mirror. Had it been a mistake to let Tara style her hair? She patted the mass of pinned curls on top of her head. Would Corbin think she was trying too hard?

The bedroom door opened against the wall. "Jess, you in here? I'm a little late, but I'll be ready in a—"

She stepped from the bathroom and whatever else Corbin had been about to say tumbled silently from his open jaw. Jessie squeezed her eyes shut in sudden humiliation. This was ridiculous. She should've never listened to Tara.

"Wow … you're beautiful."

Stunned, she opened her eyes and searched for signs of sarcasm. Corbin stared at her in admiration. She touched her hair then plucked at her green sweater. "You don't think it's too much?"

A slow smile lifted his handsome mouth as he strode the distance between them. His hand caressed the soft angora fleece covering her arm. "Not. At. All."

"When are we gonna leave?" Timmy crashed into the room with Garrett on his heels.

"Yeah, I'm hungry!"

Jessie hadn't returned Corbin's touch before. But his response, along with advice from Tara, gave her the confidence she'd lacked. She raised her arm and let her palm rest against his chest. "I'll start the van." In deliberate, slow movements, she let her hand slide to the side and across his arm.

Alyssa, I'm evening the playing field.

Chapter Twenty One

Jessie loaded the cake roll and cookies she'd baked into the van. Although she looked forward to the Christmas party, the thought of Alyssa flirting with Corbin churned her insides.

Alyssa's flawless skin, straight blonde hair, and pre-childbirth figure made her look as if she came out of a beauty magazine—not to mention the way she walked. If Jessie tried moving her hips that way, she'd run into every doorway in her house.

"Humpf." Jessie planted her hands on the van floor beside the cookies. Though she didn't battle weight, her dark hair and shorter height definitely contrasted to Alyssa's angelic appearance. *If people only knew.* She nabbed one of the cookies and leaned against the open back hatch. Crumbs tumbled onto her sweater as she nibbled on the chocolate edge. Envy wasn't of the Lord. But neither was adultery, or whatever Alyssa had in mind.

"God, help me get through this evening and keep my claws retracted." She rose from situating the baked goods and, out of habit, tried to toss her hair behind her shoulder. "Oh," she'd forgotten about the up-do Tara had styled for her.

She closed the door and glanced at her reflection. Satisfied she had an edge, Jessie moved toward the front of the van.

Conviction nudged her heart. Why was she worried about having an edge with the Lord on her side? Jesus Christ would battle for her. *Help me not get in the way ... and help Alyssa draw to You ... and not my husband.* She couldn't resist adding the last part.

The door to the house opened and the kids filed out, followed by Corbin. A light scent of cologne wafted through the air sending a giddy sensation through Jessie's body. He was *her* husband. She'd stick to his side like glue. Alyssa wouldn't have a chance.

Not long after they walked through Wade and Vera's door, the children found the table of food and a friend tugged Jessie toward a group of women. She gave a backward glance to Corbin who nodded understandingly.

If only he'd held her hand, she wouldn't have been as easy to snatch.

Sorry, God. I shouldn't blame him. She'd awakened disappointed two mornings in a row to find Corbin sleeping on his side ... away from her.

Jessie halfway listened while keeping her antennae out for Corbin.

"You'll have to stop by and see the bedroom. It looks great!"

Jessie blinked and slowly caught up to Crystal's conversation. "I'm really glad you're happy with it."

"Oh, look, Pictionary!" Crystal pointed to the side of the room. "I love it when Vera sets out these old games. Come on, you can be my partner."

Despite her resolve to stay with Corbin, Jessie relaxed with the fun evening, consumed in games and laughter, often in a separate room.

Over an hour later, Tara squeezed through to Jessie's side. "What, may I ask, are you doing over here with Corbin over there?"

Jessie's eyes darted toward the other room. "Where is she?"

"Exactly where you think."

Anger hardened inside Jessie. If she didn't know better, she'd be certain steam was rolling from her ears.

"Hey, I see that look in your eyes. The girl's probably not a Christian yet, so don't take her life."

Jessie ignored Tara's effort to lighten her mood. "Christian or not, Alyssa should know to leave well enough alone," she half whispered. "Can't she accept Corbin's no longer available?"

"Just chill. I told you I'd take care of it. I stopped by here so you could see it happen."

Jessie didn't understand but was more than willing to see what her friend was talking about. Outside the dining room, with a bowl in his hand, Corbin stood beside Brock with Alyssa a few feet away.

"Wow, this is surprisingly good. I'll have to ask Jessie to make these."

Jessie nudged Tara. "What did you feed him?"

"Seasoned kale chips. Just wait and you'll see why—"

Corbin laughed at something Brock said and Alyssa's face wilted. Jessie looked closer and slapped a hand over her mouth to cover her giggle. "What's wrong with his smile?"

"Dry kale." Tara hooted beside her. "It gets between your teeth something awful."

Corbin made eye contact with Jessie and motioned for her to join him. "Hey, honey, you have to try what someone brought. I've never had them."

The term of endearment lost some of its power from his green speckled grin, but Jessie was too pleased with Tara's dish to let it bother her. With Alyssa gone, she stepped close to his side and reached toward the bowl.

Corbin took a drink of punch and all but one offending bit of green washed away.

"Oh, look you two, mistletoe." Someone pointed toward Jessie.

Jessie spun around. Where ever it was, she didn't want anything to do with the dreaded foliage. It only trapped people in uncomfortable situations. She instinctively took a step back.

Corbin grunted as she bumped into him. "Anxious to get started, huh?"

"What?" She glanced up. They stood directly beneath the mistletoe. "Uh, no."

She turned to the crowded room. "I don't … I mean we …*we* don't like to show public affection. It makes our kids uncomfortable."

"It's not right to fib." Corbin's breath tickled her ear. His arms came around her before she knew

233

what to do and turned her to face him. "Pretend to like it." His eyes softened as they stared into hers.

Jessie's heart thudded with the beat of a thousand drummer boys. How long had she imagined what it would be like to kiss Corbin? *Pretend?* Hardly.

Her breath shortened as he leaned forward. A vibrant mirth danced in his eyes. It must be from the gaiety of the party … or was he as happy with the situation as she was?

Jessie's eyes automatically closed as he pressed against her back, drawing them together. His warm lips moved against hers, belying a barely controlled passion. Jessie's limbs weakened as she melted against him.

A murmur rose from the room. Then someone bellowed, "No wonder they don't kiss in public." A roar of laughter followed before Corbin finished the kiss. Breathless, Jessie stared into his eyes.

The rest of the evening seemed to float by on a cloud. No matter who struck up conversation with her, Jessie made sure she was never more than a few feet away from Corbin. And each time she looked over at him, his eyes were already locked onto her.

Would he try to hold her tonight? Jessie wouldn't deny him. Not after that kiss. She touched the rim of her glass to her lips, reminiscing the feel of him so close to her. Why had they waited this long?

Because he didn't love her … and didn't want to.

***

Jessie slipped beneath the covers in the darkened room. Was Corbin already asleep? It had taken longer than normal to settle the kids into bed. Layla had been the worst. Now fully excited for Christmas, she'd talked nonstop about what might be beneath the tree.

Without a sound from her husband, Jessie rolled to her side. A weight built in her chest until it became so painful a tear slipped from her eye. How could he sleep after what happened between them? Had he wished it was Alyssa he'd kissed instead? She knew not to wander in vain imaginations, but what explanation was there for his silence?

The bed creaked and the mattress sank. Jessie held her breath. Was he moving toward her?

Corbin's chest pressed against Jessie's back, and his hand slid over her arm. He moved again, this time as if rising on his elbow. With the lightest touch, his lips grazed her arm over and over, from above her wrist toward her shoulder. Corbin moved his hand over the spots as if to rub them in, then rested his chin on her arm.

"I think you should know ... I've fallen in love with my wife."

Epilogue

The doorbell rang, and Jessie hurried to the door. With Christmas only a few days away, excitement hung in the air like the icicles on the gutter. She and Corbin had shopped smart for the kids and still had enough left over to buy for those at the shelter. The thrill of watching the residents open their gifts last night had kept a constant smile in her heart all through the evening.

Layla crowded around her as the door swung wide. Heather stood on the porch holding something wrapped in a towel.

"Merry Christmas."

"Merry Christmas to you, too."

She handed the package to Jessie. "Dale and I wanted to do something for you to show you how—" Tears clouded Heather's eyes as she choked back a sob, "to show you how much we appreciate all you've done. I don't know where we'd be right now if not for you guys."

Layla bounced back into the house as Corbin crowded the door beside Jessie. His kind eyes met hers as she accepted the large, round gift. Something pricked her palms as she pulled back the corner of the towel, exposing the smell of evergreen. "Oh, how beautiful." Swatches of pine and cedar lay wired together with small ornaments and ribbon glued in a circle.

"We made it together, me, Dale, and the kids."

"It's beautiful. Don't you think so, Corbin?"

"Perfect." He lifted it from her hands. "In fact, I think it should go right here." He removed a welcome sign that hung beside the door and hooked the wreath over a nail.

"Today's Dale's last day in the city." Heather smiled more brightly than Jessie could remember. "Thank you so much for the job. He's excited to start working for you. And I'm glad you talked us into staying at the shelter. Not only did we get Sissy to stay there too, we've saved enough money for an apartment!"

Jessie grabbed her in a hug. "I'm so happy for you!"

"Me, too. I finally feel like I can breathe again." She wiped a tear from the corner of her eye. "We could've never done this without you. I know God's been with me the whole time, acting through both of you."

Jessie swallowed a lump in her throat as Heather traced her steps back to her car. God had been with her and Corbin, too, bringing them closer and uniting them the way He designed marriage to be.

Corbin reached for her hand, something he'd been doing a lot lately, while they waved good-bye. The cold concrete of the porch registered with Jessie's stocking covered feet and sent a shiver through her frame.

"You cold?" A sensual note hung in Corbin's voice.

"Uh huh." She smiled knowingly, and despite the ring of the phone from inside the house, inched closer to him.

"I know just the thing," he placed her hands around his neck and bent his head toward hers, "to warm you up."

Jessie sighed as her body fell against his. Their lips touched at the same time Shannon called from the living room. "Mom, Dad?"

Footsteps reverberated inside the house before the door swung open. "Eww, gross!"

###

A Note from the Author

Thank you for joining me in this new series. Jessie and Corbin's story was so fun to write. Several of the humorous moments stem from my own family's adventures, such as the limestone mints, Jessie and the couch (To my surprise, it actually worked and no busted lip!), and the cards at Samantha's party to name a few.

I hope you'll join me in Book Two of the After the Vows series where we'll follow up with Tara and Justin. They don't know it yet, but they're about to fall in love again—with each other!

Please remember, reviews help my stories reach a wider audience. So if you have the time, please consider leaving one at your favorite online store. I enjoy hearing from my readers and can be found at www.reginatittel.com, or you can leave me a message at reginatittel@gmail.com.

God bless you,

Regina Tittel